THE LOST BROTHERHOOD

*To Jean,
with love

Harrison*

Harrison Hickman

Published by New Generation Publishing in 2016

Copyright © Harrison Hickman 2016

First Edition

The author asserts the moral right under the Copyright, Designs and Patents Act 1988 to be identified as the author of this work.

All Rights reserved. No part of this publication may be reproduced, stored in a retrieval system or transmitted, in any form or by any means without the prior consent of the author, nor be otherwise circulated in any form of binding or cover other than that which it is published and without a similar condition being imposed on the subsequent purchaser.

www.newgeneration-publishing.com

Forward

For me, *The Lost Brotherhood* is more than just a science fiction dystopian novel. It was a personal journey exploring modern society. How does it truly work? Who makes the decisions? How do ordinary people react to those decisions?

I wrote this book during the summer of 2009. Many things were happening in the UK and around the world. The government was in crisis over the Expenses Scandal. Swine Flu was whipping up media headlines. When I finally completed the novel at the end of August, I felt relief and panic at the same time. Was it worthy of the dystopian family? Who would want to read it? The truth is: I don't know the answers to either of these questions.

The Lost Brotherhood is my attempt to make sense of the chaotic world we live in. I placed my antihero, Benedict Nettlefold, into a world where bureaucrats are gods, where violence is a way of life, where being stabbed in the back is a routine occurrence.

I have many people to thank for helping with this book:

Noel Boyd, for helping to edit this book and improve the plot.

Critics at various creative writing groups I have had the privilege of being part of over the years. Even those who didn't read any of this book helped to improve my writing.

Members of the Glasgow writing community who have given me the courage to keep going despite the odds. I am indebted to them from pulling me back from the brink of putting my pen down.

Lastly, of course, to my family.

Chapter 1   Royalty, etc.

Through the snow-blown hills, across the grassy fields, along the dark empty roads, a gentle breeze echoed, spilling its way over flowerbeds and swimming like a gigantic eel through the black forests. Atop a particular flower, there was this yellow butterfly, obviously quite asleep. Suddenly a gust of wind blew the tiny thing off the flower and upwards. The butterfly fought the wind currents, eventually managing to collapse onto a black rock. It saw the lights up ahead – the glow of a tiny hamlet. It seemed a cosy little place.

There was a small pub in there, its doors covered in vines. The pub was ancient, in use since the days of Lady Joanne.

Many old men used to remember hearing tales and legends about her that their fathers told them – how she used to walk through the country lanes with a dream in her head of a peaceful world. If you could speak to them, you would hear how they'd wonder what she was like when their fathers showed them pictures of her that were always kept in a chest placed high on a shelf.

But Lady Joanne was long since dead, the day of her passing clearly marked when she set up the twenty-four brotherhoods. Each one was responsible for the up keeping of the planet.

Apart from one, all had fallen from grace. And the one that still stood was the Epsilon Brotherhood – protectors and guardians together. Their warriors, generals and sergeants were scattered far and wide.

And one of them was in this pub.

His name was Benedict Nettlefold and he was a tall, young lad who sat hunched over on the stool. He was finishing his pipe, scraping the last tobacco remnants into the ashtray.

Benedict was a commander – but would have been a general had he not been ruined. He'd worked long and hard for that commission, but at the last moment he'd been ruined... completely.

This was what the Epsilon Brotherhood was made of – not all, but most: disgraced people.

And Benedict was just another one of them.

As he fumbled around for another tobacco pouch, he realised that all he was... was remains. Remains of what he could have been. Remains of what he *should* have been.

But these remains were on a mission; not a major one, just a normal arrest – a youth well known round here for causing trouble.

Reaching inside his jacket, he made sure his gun was at the ready.

He said to the barman: "Another pint of ale please." As he handed over the money, the door opened.

This was it.

Benedict whipped out the gun and pointed it at the new arrival. "On your knees, mate," he snarled. But then his terror stopped when he recognised the royal symbol on the stranger's robe.

"If you would care not to shoot me, Commander, I was told I'd find you here. You'd better come with me immediately – there's an important meeting and you're needed."

"Wait a minute!" said Benedict, chuckling. "Important? Sorry to tell you that I don't have a high rank: I'm just a commander and I'm here to do a job." He put the gun away.

"Well," said the stranger, removing his hood, "I do apologise – but this youth you're after can wait, I'm afraid. There are other commanders, Benedict."

"Don't I recognise you from somewhere?" said Benedict. "Oh, that's right! You're the Minuet – I read about you last week. 'The biggest fraud on the planet' they referred to you as."

The Minuet rolled his eyes: "There's a car outside, commander… if you care to follow me."

"Wait a minute," said Benedict, clicking his tongue loudly, "I ain't following anyone anywhere! Ya got it? I don't follow anyone – not even His Majesty."

"There's a commission in it for you," said the Minuet.

Suddenly Benedict was filled with a fresh sense of self: a commission? He could use one of those – well, he did have one… well, nearly a commission. It *would* be a shame not to jump at this opportunity.

"Alright," said Benedict. "Alright, Minuet; let me buy you a drink."

"I can't," he replied. "We're due at the palace."

And so they left of the pub, Nettlefold keeping an eye all around him – the criminal would be here in a moment or so: it was his job to stop him – even if the Minuet didn't approve of it…

"So," continued the Minuet as they neared the rich-looking car, "are you fully aware of the terms and conditions?"

"Oh, fucking hell – course I am. Why wouldn't I be?"

"It's a modern world, Commander."

"Of course: that's why I know about these fucking 'terms and conditions'…"

The Minuet scowled at him silently. "Just agree with the Terms and Conditions Protocol…"

"I agree," grumbled Benedict.

"And please mind your language as well," said the Minuet, "especially when we're in the presence of His Majesty."

"I suppose the best bit of the job's going to be the bit when we're on some sort of flying machine, most likely one of those clinically obese zeppelins."

"For once we are in agreement; the ship we've got is quite unlike anything else we have."

"Which ship is it then?"

"You'll get told at the palace," said the Minuet – he seemed quite eager to be away from this place.

"Just tell me what ship we're using," said Benedict. "Or I ain't going…"

"Captain Sender's *Levitator*," answered the Minuet.

"Never heard of that ship," commented Benedict.

"She isn't a zeppelin," informed the Minuet. "She's one of the new fleet."

"You mean…"

"Yes, Mr Nettlefold," the Minuet replied. "Fresh from the shipyard – built by – "

"I don't want to know who built it," said Benedict annoyed, "I just wanna know if it's safe."

"Of *course* it's safe," the Minuet interjected. "Don't worry, Mr Nettlefold. Don't worry: the tests have confirmed that she is safe to use. Captain Sender himself had the pilots take him on a tour of Russia in it. Do not worry," he continued. "Do not worry – the pilots have been trained 'til their sick and tired of it."

"Right then," said Benedict Nettlefold, "if that's that – then we'd better be going."

The Minuet opened the door for Benedict who sat inside reluctantly – that criminal and *that* ship were simply too much for him.

The car was started and the driver took them away down the country lane. As they were about to turn onto the main highway, a gunshot made all their blood run cold.

"Shit," muttered Benedict, taking out his gun. The car stopped. "Sorry, Minuet," he whispered back at the royal figure. He hurled himself out of the car, holding his gun in front of him.

The criminal was midway across the field, dashing like hell away from the car.

"That bleeding bastard must've fired a shot at us," he reported, "then made a run for it. Well – not time for dwelling on moralities now."

Benedict raised the pistol and fired a shot. It missed, skimming past his head and striking a distant tree, causing a puff-like sound to ring through the field.

"Fuck!" cried Benedict. "That bastard got away." He aimed to fire again, but discovered too quickly that the gun was empty.

"Horseshit!" he barked to himself, jabbing in several new acid-loaded bullets and slamming the barrel into place.

Slowly and aiming carefully, he fired again.

It hit the criminal in the back of the neck – the youth screamed in agony as the magic bullet released its deadly load. The youth clawed for some strange reason at the decaying flesh on his scalp, ripping it off like paper.

Another shot later, he was dead.

Nettlefold smiled: "Another day's work nicely done…"

He got into the car, shutting the door next to him. The driver took them away from the scene. Benedict didn't look back at all, as the dead youth dissolved into the earth like salt in water.

The palace was the same as it had always been: bright orange, with the bricks laid neatly in concrete. The walls were polished to achieve a kind of sparkly look – although marble was difficult to get these days: the world had changed too much.

Nevertheless, the front gardens were done up in grand form – foreign shrubs littered the crevices between the paths and grass. A servant cleaned these paths that the king liked to stroll down with important guests, particularly ones from Pacifica and Africa.

And with this new fleet of ships on the way, it was important that other countries and nations had their greatest scientists and professors donate their knowledge for possible improvements to these new ships.

Of course, the king had one of the new fleet built just for him: the *Champion*. The heavy ship had taken several months to actually construct and several years to get off the ground. The reason for this was that the iridium absorbing sheet in the engine couldn't be hammered properly into shape – but it turned out that there were so many impurities in it that they had to extract a whole new block of iridium altogether. To make matters worse, the highly trained pilots that had been selected from millions of competitors were so disappointed at the entire ordeal that they considered not piloting it at all and finding another flying activity to pass their time. However, in the due course of time, the iridium foil was eventually fixed and the test flight took place.

It took a while for the pilots to get used to the controls – despite their training: you see, these new ships weren't at all like zeppelins: the engines that generated the super light particles needed to be reset every one thousand metres the ship climbed or descended. It was like the gear system in a car, except the "gears" in these new ships went up to over sixty.

That wasn't even half the difficulty.

These ships tended to be about fifty times faster that zeppelins, so the pilots weren't used to such speeds – for thousands of years, it seemed as though man had never gone so fast.

Their training didn't teach them that.

As well as the fact that because of the rotation of the engine, the super light particles tended to crash into the side of the compartment, meaning that the pilot needed to adjust the steering every so often – and because of this, he needed to reset the engine.

There was all this and a hell of a lot more techniques and strategic steering moves to learn – as well as achieving the confidence to fly the damn thing.

However, the king was confident that the *Champion* would be his new flagship – and soon, the entire world would be filled with these ships. These new ships had an official designation (a long and very boring name), but they were known to the common tongue as the *Champion* Class.

Benedict Nettlefold got out of the car, with pretence at difficulty, for he tired of royalty. Many years ago, when he passed the academic examinations, he was introduced to His Majesty along with all the other successful candidates and invited to a feast. The amount of food they served! Quite literally fit for a king.

But when a member of this newly-discovered royalty turned on him, Benedict had lost much interest in it: the king was now a man in rich, purple robes: not the adventurous, youthful figure that children made him out to be.

"So this is the palace," he commented grimly, watching the Minuet struggle getting out of the car due to the big, black belt he wore, hanging of him. Benedict had taken out a cigarette and wedged it between his lips. He lit a match.

"Yes it is," the Minuet said loudly – indicating that Benedict should put the match out.

"That wasn't a question." Benedict reluctantly dropped the match to the ground and stamped on it, snuffing out the flame. He slid the fag into his pocket.

"It sounded like one. Anyway," continued the Minuet, "come this way."

They passed through the gardens, Benedict ignoring the wonderful display of foreign flowers completely: there *were* other matters at hand. As soon as this thing with the king was over, he needed to get back to the body (or what remained of it) and take have the cops take it away for pathologist to examine.

Nevertheless, he seemed patient as they made their way through the softly carpeted corridors, up the carpeted stairwells, to the carpeted floor in which His Majesty resided most of the time.

The Minuet let Benedict into a cramped room with several chairs slammed against the stiff wall. "Wait here," he said, "while I go and tell His Majesty that you are here."

He watched the royalty go – desperately wanting to make a comment, but this *was* the palace: they wouldn't be much appreciated here.

Benedict reflected over the past few years: what a ride it had been – and it could've been much, much better. If that stupid bastard hadn't spoiled it for him, then he could have been a commissioned general, with his own private army – God, it would've been like a country of his own: the ability to tell others not only what to do, but to live, sleep, and eat by his laws.

And he had worked for it, putting the effort in over the years. He'd nearly got there; nearly, nearly, nearly…

But then someone called Dr Macintyre, who disliked commander a great deal for many unknown reasons, decided to make up a story about him (something to do with a non-existent threat he'd made to a family). His commission had been ripped from under him – right from under his feet. To make matters worse, it had been at the award ceremony itself at his wedding! Dr Macintyre had come right into the church with several police and one horrid detective and taken Benedict away on site.

Now he was left a mere commander – several ranks away from a general, and only a few ranks up from a captain. He spent his career doing menial jobs for the police instead, ones that involved catching youths or shooting killers: that was his job now.

He knew that the king had called him here for a reason – and what could that possibly be?

A steward entered the room with a bowl of pebbles – he poured them into a plant on the windowsill above Benedict and then began to leave again; as he was on the way out, he turned to him and said:

"I know you! You're the sergeant convicted of threatening to rape and murder a family, aren't you? Well, we don't want any of your kind here, mate."

Benedict was enraged. So much that he grabbed the steward by the collar and took his gun from his coat, pointing it at the steward's chest.

"I'm a *commander*," Benedict snarled menacingly at him, "not a fucking sergeant! I want you to repeat that before you go to bed tonight: Commander Benedict Nettlefold. Is that understood?"

"Yes sir," replied the steward, now slightly afraid.

"Now get out, you arrogant piece of shit!"

The steward bowed out of shear terror, and slowly, like the ticking of an hour hand, exited the room.

Benedict sat down, still angry, feeling a familiar shiver in his heart: the sight of the church doors being flung open and Dr Macintyre storming in with those police. Shaking himself free of this, he replaced his gun into his coat and took a cigarette out of his pocket – but then he remembered that he *was* in a palace.

"Got to watch my health," he muttered quietly, replacing the cigarette.

"Excuse me," said a new voice.

Benedict Nettlefold was struck with fear at the thought the butler was standing there, but as he looked into the doorway, he noticed a familiar royal figure. No, not the king, but his royal advisor: the Patrician.

Without question, he stood up straight and bowed his head. "Good day, Mr Patrician," he said respectably.

The royal figure had his moustache and beard neatly trimmed and wore the clipped suit that tied itself tightly to him. The Patrician walked around Benedict Nettlefold, studying the young commander in detail.

"King Christopher is waiting for you," he said. "He wants to send a mission, you know. Apparently, he wishes to investigate the strangest attacks I've heard – attacks in Pacifica. It'll be an epic adventure for you, Commander: young lads such as yourself need one. I just thought I'd tell you." He paused. "Down the hall," he continued, "then take a left."

"Thank you, Mr Patrician," said Benedict, bowing. "And I bid you a good evening, sir."

"You as well," said the Patrician. He left the room, leaving Benedict to make his own way.

"Thank you again."

One might expect that this was a comment of deep sarcasm – but when Nettlefold talked about the Patrician, he never dared to be sarcastic. The Patrician was feared – often more than King Christopher.

Benedict Nettlefold followed the Patrician's directions. He strolled leisurely down the long corridor, gazing at old pictures left and right, not as interested as an artist or writer; he passed a very mean-looking golden statue and noticed the corridor to the left. He took it and soon arrived at the pink coloured set of doors with gold vine wrapped through the handles. He scratched his stubble nervously as he slowly opened it.

Inside, at a large, circular table, sat several individuals:

One was a rich-looking gentleman in a uniform – a general by the number of stripes. He possessed a ginger pile of hair combed neatly to the side and had his moustache very neatly trimmed. This general had at least twenty medals emblazoned on his uniform – most gold. Here was someone who'd worked their way up through life and studies – someone who Benedict Nettlefold could have been, but wasn't, because of that worthless bastard who'd stopped him.

Next to him sat a younger fellow, blond, in his twenties who was a commander. His hands were rested on the table, his fingers interlocked. Two silver medals were also fixed on his uniform: this was exactly the sort of person Benedict hated. He was young, and yet he'd been able to have this most splendid privilege of wearing his pride without *any* proper life experience. Yet Nettlefold had worked his ass off for it and got nothing in return, aside from the knowledge he was now a rapist – but he knew he wasn't.

No, Benedict Nettlefold hated this young man from first sight. He hated him so much that what happened later would affect how he behaved on perhaps the wildest adventure ever dreamt of.

Across from them both sat the Minuet in all his splendid glory.

And next to him, with over sixty golden medals pinned to his tunic, sat King Christopher himself.

Chapter 2 The Meeting

Benedict Nettlefold continued to gaze at the group sitting before him.

He bowed before King Christopher: "Your Majesty," he whispered with deep respect. "A good evening to you."

"Benedict Nettlefold," said the king. "It is good to see you. Please take a seat over there if you please."

"Thank you, Majesty." Benedict sat down next to the Minuet, trying to ignore the young commander.

"Now," said King Christopher, "I would like to introduce you to these gentlemen. This is General Burt Mickson," he said, pointing to the man with about twenty medals. "General, this is Commander Benedict Nettlefold."

"Good to meet you, commander," replied Mickson, reaching his hand out to Nettlefold.

King Christopher, then indicated the younger man: "This is Commander Justin Collington."

Now, Benedict Nettlefold was hesitant: with disgust and hate, he shook hands with Collington.

"I've heard about some of your work," said Collington. "You've done some good advances for this country."

"I only do menial missions – in fact, jobs, commander. I'm not part of the advancing column."

"Now that you both are acquainted to Commander Nettlefold," said the king, "we can begin. General Mickson…"

"Majesty," said the general, standing up and making his way to a large map of the world on the wall. He put his fat little finger on Central Asia.

"About three months ago," he said, "something happened here; in this little village called Ulanva – the locals described what happened as horrendous: a freakish lighting storm erupted."

"Why do you deem it as suspicious, sir?" enquired Nettlefold.

"It wasn't the lightening," said the general, "but the energy detected. It… well, one *could* describe it as a negative light we observed. Black light, to be more precise."

"So where is this leading, sir?" asked Commander Nettlefold.

"The mysterious fact is that the storm originated from Pacifica," informed Mickson. "We managed to trace it back there – and pinpoint its exact point of origin. We intend to investigate it. The mission will be to penetrate the island…"

"You want to penetrate Pacifica, sir?"

"Yes, Mr Nettlefold."

"But you can't just do that – those people have got rights too, sir; and besides, we don't want *another* war with them."

"I would be most grateful if you didn't mention that," said General Mickson. "Understood? Very well then. Now, to continue: We will penetrate the island and land in the rainforest. Once there, the detectives and our physicist will be able to examine the energy more closely."

"Why detectives, sir?" Benedict asked. "Why not have more physicists?"

"Because, we require people bound by the government," explained Mickson. "I don't want it falling into the hands of civilians – besides, both our detectives are qualified in a large area of physics. They'll know what they're looking for."

"When you say 'both'," replied Nettlefold, "you mean that there are only two detectives coming? Listen, sir, if you intend for this mission to take place, you need *more* than two of them. What's the crew compliment by the way?"

"Well," replied Commander Collington, "there's us; also, the Minuet; fifty other Epsilon soldiers; a professor who's our physicist; two detectives; also the captain of the

Levitator, of which I'm sure you're familiar with, and his crew; and lastly, our chief medic."

"Who's the medic?" inquired Benedict.

"It's," Collington stared heavenwards trying to remember, "a Dr Philip Macintyre."

"What?!" snarled Commander Nettlefold suddenly, completely forgetting that King Christopher was in the room too. He turned towards His Majesty: "I do apologise, Excellency, for my words were too loud for this palace."

"Apology accepted," smiled the king, "but you must understand why Dr Macintyre is on this mission."

"Why is that, Majesty?"

"Philip is very experienced in missions like these," informed General Mickson, forming a ring with his thumb and first finger to lay down his point. "I believe that with his assistance, we can make the entire operation a success."

He was on first name basis with the doctor? It was bad enough being on professional terms with him: it made one wonder how anyone as rich as a general would get to know someone as insane as Macintyre. It was bad enough that he was a doctor – but when you get one of these stupid individuals and give him a high rank in the medical core – then you've got a problem.

"But, sir," said Nettlefold through gritted teeth, "you only need a few nurses – you don't need a doctor."

"As I said," continued Mickson, "we do require him – he knows exactly what he's doing; trust me…"

He knows what he's doing? Nettlefold didn't even need to drive down Memory Lane to understand why one shouldn't trust that son-of-a-bitch.

"Gentlemen," coughed the Minuet from the side, "back to the mission, if you please…"

"Of course," replied the general, casting an annoyed eye at Nettlefold. "The *Levitator* will take us over Europe, through Russia, and then deep into Asia." He gestured at the map, again prodding it with his finger. "We will make a stop at the Edge of Asia before making our way across the Pacific Ocean to Pacifica, where, as I told you, we will land deep within the island where we will attempt to find out more about this energy."

"Can I ask a question, sir?"

"Yes, Mr Nettlefold."

"What *exactly* is my job on the mission?"

"Well," said General Mickson, "it's quite obvious. You're a soldier – "

"That's where you're wrong, sir," replied Benedict. "I am a soldier, yes; however I'm not part of the advancing column. I have little interest – "

"Can you fight?" asked the Minuet suddenly.

"Of course I can fight!" exclaimed Benedict Nettlefold. "I can!"

"Then that's all you need to do," said Mickson. "If we run into any trouble, you just need to take out your weapon and shoot. What's more complicated than that?"

"Once this mission is over," said Commander Collington, "you can begin – "

"You're assuming," said Nettlefold, "that I'm going on the mission."

General Mickson paused uneasily, glancing at the king, and with his assurance, said quietly:

"Benedict Nettlefold: I regret to inform you that you have no choice in the matter."

"What?" Nettlefold shrieked. "You're talking no sense at all! Are you saying that I must be transported on the *Levitator* against my will?"

"Yes," Mickson replied flatly.

"We thought it was in your best interest, commander," said King Christopher.

"But, Majesty: I have a lot of work to do here."

"That's what the police are for, Mr Nettlefold," replied the king. "You've been doing the wrong job."

"But why me?" pleaded Benedict. "Why am I so special?"

General Mickson looked uneasily at the king. "Should I tell him, Majesty?"

"Yes."

"What do you mean?" Benedict inquired, deeply puzzled.

"Dr Macintyre asked me to bring you," said General Mickson. "He said that he wanted his eye on you, and couldn't do such a thing while he was outside Great Britain."

Benedict was furious: that complete bastard, Macintyre, had now restricted his freedom. First it was his commission; now, this 'professional doctor' had now started to control his daily movements. What was the next stage? Telling him how to eat and sleep? By God, Benedict had had enough of that crap: day in, day out, the filthy lot that was the medical profession, victimised people with any slight emotional problems, and made their life a living hell.

By God, if Benedict was in charge of things, he'd have Macintyre and the rest of the gang strung up like puppets.

"So this is all Dr Macintyre's idea of a job, sir?" said Nettlefold. "Well – I wouldn't be surprised," he whispered.

"I heard that!" snapped Mickson. "I want a word with you after the meeting."

"Yes sir."

"You should show more respect for that man!" snarled General Mickson, now thoroughly annoyed. "There's nothing about him that makes him an outlaw – and I will not have him spoken about like that."

"Can we please move on?" groaned the Minuet.

"Yes; my apologies," said Mickson. "Mr Collington; if you please…"

"Yes sir," the young commander replied. He took Mickson's place and the general took a well-earned seat at the table.

"Weapons wise," said Collington, "we want to travel quite light. Each Epsilon soldier will carry their own personal weapon with enough ammunition to kill twenty souls each. However, the *Levitator* is equipped to deal with larger threats. As is custom, security onboard the *Levitator* will all be armed. *Should* we run into any threats beyond which we can fight with the weapons for the mission, the *Levitator* has an emergency weapons compartment filled with rifles, grenades, etc.

"As far as food and water are concerned, the *Levitator* will provide hot and cold meals, tea, coffee, water, and emergency rations, should they be required. As General Mickson has mentioned, Dr Macintyre will foresee the medical side of things – so he will be in charge of the medical supplies – both stored and emergency.

"On the accommodation side of things: the Epsilon soldiers and security will share rooms between two – however, we shall all be allocated in our own individual rooms. Also in individual rooms will be Dr Macintyre, the professor, the detectives, etc. Captain Sender and his officers will have their own allocated rooms. The rooms themselves are all the same size – but they are fairly large each.

"There is a conference room onboard the ship for meetings about the mission: it will mainly be used by Captain Sender and his officers for meetings regarding the ships operations – however, it is suitable for use for any meeting: from the small security team meetings to larger meetings which involve the procedures we face when arriving at Pacifica.

"Are there any questions?"

"When do we leave?" Benedict asked.

"Three weeks' time," replied the Minuet. "Commander Collington will be in charge of arrangements."

"Very well then, gentlemen, if that is all," said the king, "I bid you goodnight."

All present bowed before King Christopher and left the room. The Minuet muttered a few words to Commander Collington, then retired to his quarters.

"Commander," said Collington, holding a piece of paper in his hand, "these are the arrangements: I've written them down for you – I'll meet you outside your house at

03:00 on the morning of departure in my car and drive you to the airport."

"Thank you, Commander," said Nettlefold, watching the young man leave. He stuffed the paper in his pocket. As he turned to go himself, General Mickson coughed behind him.

"Mr Nettlefold, a word in my royal study, if you please."

Grudgingly, Benedict followed Mickson down several flights of stairs. His office was located on the bottom floor, the door concealed with plants growing out of ancient china pots. Inside were pictures of historical campaigns against the outlaws and evil dictators that had threatened the planet – but all the good generals had gone.

Mickson ordered Benedict to stand before his mahogany desk, while he shut the door behind him. The general was quite silent until he had seated himself.

"Just what the hell were you up to, commander?!" he snarled. "How dare you talk about Dr Macintyre like that! Just who d'you think you're talking about?"

"Permission to reply, sir."

"Granted."

"With respect sir, you can tell Dr Macintyre to get himself out of this country and sell himself to the Bikini Atoll!"

General Mickson was apoplectic. He vociferated: "Don't you dare talk about him like that again! Don't you fucking dare!"

"That bastard ruined my goddam career!"

"He did what was right –"

"He fucked up big time!"

"Do not speak like that about him," Mickson growled. "I am warning you…"

"Then maybe he should have some respect then," said Benedict. "Not just for me; but for the rest of the Epsilon Brotherhood."

"How dare you speak like that about him? What in God's name is going through your head - "

"Excuse me - "

"Do not interrupt me when I'm speaking!" barked the general. "Have some fucking respect!"

"Tell that to Dr Macintyre - "

"Shut the fuck up!"

"Do not tell me to shut up, sir!" yelled Nettlefold. "It's Dr Macintyre who you need to tell to shut up – he's the stupid fucker round here!"

"That's one of my friends you're talking about, my good man!" stuttered Mickson. "If he ruined you career, then he must have had some *God damn fucking reason to do so*!"

Benedict's blood had passed beyond boiling point. Without thinking about his actions, he took his gun from his overcoat and pointed it at Mickson's chest.

"Now you're silent," sneered Benedict.

"Do you realise that I could have you reported for this," said General Mickson. "You'd be out the Epsilon Force before you could say your own name."

"Well, your mate Macintyre ruined my career anyway," replied Benedict, and in cocking the weapon, whispered: "So I guess it don't matter…"

"Listen, commander – "

"No, you listen, general; I joined the Epsilon Force so I could serve my country faithfully – and I still *do* love my country. So," he spat, "if try to ever lever me out of it, you're fucked." Benedict deactivated the pistol and replaced it into his pocket.

"No wonder Dr Macintyre tried to ruin you," said Mickson quietly. "You're nothing, Benedict. You're nothing more than a feeble commander fighting for your own feeble cause," he sneered. "Commander Collington though, is braver: he's got some medals. Someday, he'll make general; meanwhile, you'll still be doing menial jobs for the police. You're a fucked up man, Benedict."

Commander Nettlefold stood frozen still, his hand not touching the pistol at all.

General Mickson eyed him, spitting slightly through his teeth, said:

"Now get the fuck out of my office and go home. Commander Collington will pick you up in three weeks, so be the fuck ready then."

"Yes sir." Benedict saluted, and then marched stiffly out of the office.

If he wasn't in the palace, but somewhere else, Benedict would have broken something, but, as it was, he was in a place of royalty: a place of best behaviour: he didn't dare destroy anything here...

A guard showed him out of the palace, through the garden paths, and left him by himself on the streets. Benedict waited for a few seconds, and then trudged slowly away from the palace. As he made his way through the city, the streets became less green, and became darkened instead. The trees on the pavements were replaced with overflowing dustbins and broken bottles; the grocery and butcher shops became pubs and brothels, with the drunks and prostitutes swaggering about outside, as if that was their natural state. Suddenly the evening light became dark and pitch black with the flats either side of the road venting choking soot onto the streets.

A cry made Benedict glance to his left to see a bunch of drunks emerge from a shop selling strong spirits. Your average person would have prayed to God at that moment, but Nettlefold's God was in his coat, fully loaded with bullets.

Nettlefold glanced at his watch: quarter to ten. He'd be early for the bus; perhaps he'd have time for a chat with his friend John, who was the driver.

Commander Nettlefold took a left, then another left, and then a right, finally arriving at the derelict bus stop. Even his gun shook at this street: North Princes Street, it was called; why a prince would even come here, you could wonder at; for North Princes Street was full of drug addicts, alcoholic prostitutes, and even worse: the uneducated. Yes, there *were* other uneducated people around the city; but here was where they were focused, for North Princes Street was full of the world of neglect: litter, ash, and filthy coal that was poured on the road. It was so bad here that Lord Baxter Brickleton, the man in charge of the environmental committee, had considered turning it into a rubbish site: it was that bad. However, his fellow associates had advised him against it, for they considered the street to be "in repair stage".

It was the complete opposite of that.

The uneducated ruled this street. And they *hated* educated people, especially businessmen: God they loathed them. One would wonder why any literate person would come here in the first place. The answer was simple: the bus stop that Benedict Nettlefold was walking too was the first stop of the 751 Route: a major link with from the city to the countryside. As a law, buses couldn't stop on roadsides unless there was a bus stop there. So, as the next official bus stop for the 751 Route was on the edge of the city, these commuters had to come here.

But for now, North Princes Street seemed empty. Benedict Nettlefold trudged unevenly to the bus shelter. He took a seat under the glass and thought about the events in the palace: maybe he shouldn't have yelled at General Mickson. But then again, any bastard that supported Dr Macintyre deserved what they got: Mickson had earned it.

A movement in the corner of his eye made Benedict Nettlefold notice a panicky businessman dash towards the shelter. He looked around him, and then flopped down next to Benedict.

"Jesus, man," he said, "that was a close one!"

"What d'ya mean?" asked Nettlefold.

"I nearly ran into a gang of the uneducated," said the businessman, setting down his briefcase.

"I wouldn't do that here," said Nettlefold.

"You're right," he replied. "Guess I don't want one of them coming up to me and saying: 'Hey, Barry, give us ya briefcase, or we'll drag you into the undergrowth.'"

"I wouldn't worry," said Benedict Nettlefold. "I'm part of the Epsilon Force – don't worry: you're safe with me."

"Thanks," said the businessman. "If you've got a gun, I'll tell you my name's Barry Griffiths."

"The name's Commander Benedict Nettlefold."

"Well, commander – pleased to meet you."

Benedict Nettlefold glanced the other way, in a desperate effort to avoid Barry's eyes; his heart collapsed with agonising relief when he saw the bus coming. "It's early," he whispered quietly.

"Let's get outta here," said Barry as the bus pulled up. The driver opened the doors. The businessman pushed past Benedict and paid his fare.

Benedict ambled onto the empty bus next. He put a couple of coins into the fare box.

"Hi Ben," said the driver.

"Oh, hello John," said Commander Nettlefold. "God it's getting dark now."

"I know; soon it'll be so dark, that my mood will decay."

"I think mine's decaying already, John."

The driver smiled – but the smile vanished as he pointed out the windscreen. "Shit! Ben, look!"

The first prostitute was out; she was wearing one of those bright red shirts that hung down to her knees – barely.

"I think we'd better go, John," said Benedict. "I know you're early, but I don't think anyone else is coming."

"You're right Ben." John shut the bus doors and pulled back the steering wheel. The bus creaked slowly at first, but as he pulled the wheel closer to his stomach, it picked up speed. They passed the prostitute; anyone could see her constant laughter was caused by excessive alcohol.

They were nearing the end of North Princes Street, when they heard the first gunshot. Suddenly, there was a clatter of gunfire: aimed at the bus.

"Shit!" cried Benedict. "John, open the back window would you!"

"Are you kidding? You'll get bullets in the bus!"

"John, we haven't a choice! I need to fire shots back – so they know we're armed!"

"Alright then!"

Nettlefold took the gun from his overcoat and dashed to the back of the bus. "Keep calm, Barry," he said to the petrified businessman. John electronically opened the rear window, allowing Nettlefold to fire shots out. "Shit!" cried Benedict Nettlefold, seeing the gang chasing them. He took aim and fired randomly, but not so as to hit the prostitute.

Suddenly Commander Nettlefold noticed of the gang had an AK 47 with him.

"Everybody down!" Nettlefold screamed.

The delinquent let the gun fire, the stream of sparks showering down the street, hitting the girl, cutting her in half.

"John, get us out of here!" yelled Barry.

John pulled the wheel back as far as it would go. They accelerated out of North Princes Street – to safety.

Benedict Nettlefold lived in a small country cottage sandwiched between a brook and a hill. Often in the late spring, a farmer would stroll along the peak with his sheep, thoroughly annoying the commander below.

Even in the countryside, adrenaline was still present.

A small country road led up to it, wild flowers protruding up from the ground on either side of the tarmac. Over the years of neglect from the king, weeds had grown up through the tarmac, spreading their evil wings. In the years to come, it would be gone, a small track abandoned by its country and consumed by nature.

However, as Benedict and John strolled towards the cottage, the road was still there. Nettlefold unlocked his front door and trudged inside. John followed, shutting the door carefully behind him

The journey had been uneventful after they had escaped from North Princes Street. Barry Griffiths had gotten off in a small village they'd passed through; he'd thanked them for saving his life and then wished them all the best. Occasionally as they made their way through the countryside, a passenger or two had gotten on – but there were not many people at this time of night. Once they'd reached Benedict's home, John had exchanged places with another driver and then both he and Benedict had made their way up to the house.

And so here they were. Benedict poured them both a glass of brandy and they made their way into the living room. As John sat down on one of the leather armchairs, Benedict got himself preoccupied with trying to light the fire. He eventually managed it, and soon the warmth spread round the cold cottage.

Benedict sat himself down on the accompanying armchair, and for a while neither of them spoke.

Eventually, John broke the silence:

"So what's this about the expedition you mentioned before?"

"Well, I was in town today, because King Christopher had chosen me to go to Pacifica on a mission to find a strange type of energy – oh, I don't know, John: it's been a long time since I've done physics. At least that was what I thought…"

"Why?"

"Because that arrogant bastard, Dr Macintyre was going on that mission too; Macintyre wanted me on the mission as well – so he could keep an eye on me. You see, he doesn't want to leave his 'patients' behind while he's outta town."

"Must've been serious what he did to you."

"Of course it was fucking serious! That piece of shit ruined me, John. I've never told you what happened, did I?"

"No, you didn't."

Benedict took a slurp of his brandy and curled his hands round the glass as though it were a bible.

"You see John," he said, "five years ago, when I was in the Epsilon Force Academy, I fell in love with this girl; her name was Adeline Paulington. God, I couldn't control how I felt about her, John. Days went by, then weeks, and finally: a whole year. I couldn't bring up the guts to tell her John. So I decided to tell a consultant about it: his name was Dr Macintyre." Nettlefold hunched forward, baring his teeth. "Dr fucking Macintyre."

"What happened?"

"I told him how I felt about her, and how I needed assistance. Macintyre seemed nice at first; he gave me advice on relationships and how to confess your feelings. And you know what? His advice paid off. I told Adeline about how I felt for her – and she agreed to be with me, said she had feelings for me too. I took the commander examination when I finished the academy, and passed 'with distinction' – I got the highest mark in the academy. Anyway, this general had heard about my mark, and he invited me to sit the general examination – d'you know what, John? I passed that too.

"Anyway, by this time, Adeline and I were living together in a penthouse apartment – it wasn't soon before I proposed to her, and she accepted! God, John, I was so happy, you couldn't believe it. Anyway, this general came up to me, and suggested giving me my general commission at my wedding. That was just fantastic, John; Adeline agreed too. I couldn't believe it: I was getting married and going to receive my dream commission on the same day. Jesus Christ, how could a man ask for any more? It was just so bloody brilliant…"

Benedict put his brandy down and took his pipe from his pocket: "Want a piece of tobacco, John?"

"Yeah, thanks Ben."

Soon, both men had lit their pipes and Benedict continued:

"Well, this Dr Macintyre didn't like me; for what reasons, I don't know. He seemed kind and generous at the consultations, and didn't appear to dislike me one bit;

when he found out I was getting married, he was *shouting* congratulations at me. God, that fucking bastard; I shoulda known, John…"

"What did he do?"

"On the day of the wedding, everything went to plan. The general had arrived with the commission stripes; the guests were all there; the food was set out; no one was late. And then I waited on the altar, the general standing next to the glass case with the stripes in. And do you know what I saw coming up that aisle? The most beautiful thing ever. I remember the way her wedding dress reflected the sunlight, the way her freckled face shone so gracefully. And it wasn't just a pretty girl I was looking at: I was staring at *my* Adeline. She wanted me, John. She wanted me." John put a hand on Nettlcfold's shoulder, as his friend rubbed tears from his eyes.

"And I stood there as the priest read out the vows," Benedict continued. "I just knew that after today, I'd never feel grim again. And then suddenly the doors to the church flew open: it was Dr Macintyre with about ten soldiers. Macintyre made all the guests leave, but Adeline insisted on staying with me: nothing could get her out.

"Dr Macintyre came forward and said these very words: *Commander Benedict Nettlefold, you are here by detained from your wedding, as you have been found to be a rapist*. That's what he said to me: those exact words."

"What did Adeline do?"

"At first, she disbelieved everything the doctor said, but then Macintyre showed her a faked diary note, which said that I'd threatened to rape and murder someone. He'd somehow copied my writing and took pleasure in showing it to her. I remember a slap in my face, John. A cold, hard, fucking slap. I was dragged away to a court of inquiry and found to me guilty of 'threatening to rape and murder'. I was left a mere commander, hated by most, liked by some. But that was three years ago, John; I've done my best to move on since then. Dr Macintyre: that fucking animal. I wasn't his first victim: he preyed on students, beckoning them to consultations and ruining them; piece of fucking shit. Piece of fucking shit!" he yelled suddenly. "So here I am, in this fuckin' little cottage because of that bastard. That animal will meet its end one day. That'll be the day when someone puts a bullet in him!"

"I'm sorry about what happened," said John, "but I wouldn't advise talking about him like that, Ben; you know how high-ranking and powerful he is…"

"Thanks John; you're right: I shouldn't be shouting too loudly about him like that: some nosy pervert will report me to the authorities; Dr Macintyre'll come along and burst into my home with his bloody codswallop and take me away. He's trashed enough people already."

"Remember what happened to Lord Marius?"

"Aye, John, I do. Lord Marius: he was one of the greatest leaders in history. Two years ago, a year after Macintyre ruined me, that fucking animal ruined Lord Marius. He'd just come back from a campaign and for no reason whatsoever, that bleedin' animal just made up a falsehood about him and spread it round like butter. Poor Marius had to leave this country; no one knows where he's gone; poor bastard – it wasn't his fault; he just did his duty and served his people."

"What gives that idiot the right to go around and hurt other people?" John said, shaking his head in disbelief. "I don't know how he's got friends, but he has hundreds of them, scattered round the country – and what amazes me, Ben, is that this bastard ruined other students, long before he met you – when he was just a nurse."

"Tell you what really annoys me though, John: the fact that he's only a youngster in is thirties. Back in the academy, all the girls had the hots for 'im."

John had downed the last of his brandy. Sighing, he said quietly: "Thanks for the drink, Ben, but I've got to head home now."

"D'you need a lift?" asked Benedict. "My car's in the garage."

"Cheers, Ben; I'd appreciate that."

About an hour later, Benedict Nettlefold got back into his house: it was cold and empty now, although the fire still burned the remaining bits of wood.

Nettlefold cleared away the glasses and made himself some tea. He sat down in his deep armchair. Against his will, he climbed up the bookshelf and removed a small picture: It was a photo of him and Adeline several weeks before the doomed wedding; never in his life had he been so happy.

He replaced the photograph.

Commander Nettlefold turned on the radio to see if anything was on; but it was late, so nothing would be. But as he roamed through the many frequencies, he came across something which made his heart boil with hatred.

A medical programme. The special guest was someone called Dr Philip Macintyre.

"So, Dr Macintyre, how do *you* deal with ethnical issues whilst providing treatment?" asked the host: Dr Jordan.

The young youthful voice responded: "Well, it's not a case of *whilst* I'm providing treatment, but *if* I provide it. You see, there are many ethnical issues on the planet – and it's quite interesting understanding them. I have to make the important decision of what takes priority: their religion or their health."

"As a young ambitious doctor who's worked their way up through the medical core, do you find that your own Christianity religion can affect your judgement?"

"I try and ignore my religion and focus on the task in hand; again, this coincides with your previous question: how I deal with these ethnical issues - "

"Fuck off," snarled Benedict as he changed the frequency. "The only religion you've got is worshipping Satan."

Outside, an owl called. Benedict realised that it was time to go to bed. Three weeks later, he'd be embarking on another mission. Despite his youthful self, Benedict felt weak; not physically weak – but emotionally weak, like he was fighting a battle that could only be won by destroying both sides.

Chapter 3   The *Levitator*

A couple of nights before departure, Benedict Nettlefold sat again with John in his living room. Both possessed a steaming mug of tea, with a hint of iron in: the teapot Nettlefold had used was old, older than him; hardly anyone would use it anymore; but for Benedict, it didn't matter: he liked the taste of metal, the way it chiselled against his cheek, the sensations spreading through his jaw.

Nevertheless, John wasn't so keen; he kept reaching into his mouth, picking the bits of rusty metal off his tongue.

It was a national holiday tomorrow, so there was no bus service. People thought it weird that a 751 Route bus was parked in Nettlefold's driveway. John planned to drive it back to the garage once he'd left Nettlefold's cottage.

The two men sat in silence; not a word was said between them.

But the silence was broken, when John whispered:

"You know Benedict, I guess life can turn out funny sometimes, you know?"

"Yeah, John; I know what you mean. But I guess for my life, the shit's hit the fan; there's fuck all I can do about it now. I wonder what she's doin' know, John?"

The driver put his mug of tea on the coffee table and gazed out the window, a shocked look appearing on his face. "Ben, look who's up in the sky!" he called eagerly.

Benedict glanced out the window, and soon he had made his way up to the glass. In the sky was something moving. At first, a dark silhouette. But as he looked closer, he saw that it was the *Levitator* – probably doing a training exercise afore mission.

Ah that wondrous ship, in all its splendid beauty; the smooth, black outline of the hull, reflecting the moonlight in a shadowy glaze. The slenderness of the ship could make a man gaze for hours, her body gliding through the air, the wind rushing past her. The propellers on the stern made a distant thudding sound, like she was calling for someone to love her.

Benedict wanted to be the pilot of that ship, guiding her across the oceans, through the mountains, letting her touch the hopeless with her love. He loved that ship. He loved it.

Soon, he'd be travelling on it; on a distant journey; but only to investigate some minor energy phenomena in Pacifica.

But those early missions! Before Benedict was even born, before his great grandfather was born, before the Epsilon Brotherhood had been created, there had been missions against evil under the command of Lady Joanne – centuries ago. The world had been so much better with her around, every soldier – whether he was a mere private or a high-ranking general – had his own adventure, his own little chronicle to add to the soil of the planet.

But Lady Joanne had died long ago in the legendary Battle of the Vine. Before she died, she ordered the creation of the twenty-four brotherhoods; when they started, it was like a dream, to continue Lady Joanne's wishes for a better world – but power always destroys dreams…

John knew it was time to say it.

"Hey, Ben," he stuttered, sweeping his friend from his transfixed gaze, "I need to tell you something…"

"Yeah sure," Nettlefold replied.

"There was a programme on the radio last night, a politics show of some sort – at the end of it, there was a quick bulletin of minor stories; I emphasise the word 'minor' – it was about Dr Macintyre."

"What's that bastard got planned?"

"I mean, the presenter only said a few words about it – nothing much. Apparently, Dr Macintyre has a new consultation hospital planned."

Now Benedict was truly enraged:

"What the fuck does he think he's doing now? Shit, John, I can't fuckin' believe this. I thought this race was human – but it bloody well isn't!"

"Well they said 'planned'."

"Aye, that's what they'll tell you. That bastard'll get his way; just you see. Let's hope the contractor sees sense and tells Macintyre to screw off."

"You know, Ben – I hope this mission is successful."

In all his rage, Nettlefold had forgotten the nervousness he'd felt in the past few days. "Aye, I hope it does; God help me if it don't work out." Suddenly he laughed: "Hey, John, do you know what Commander Collington said during the briefing? He told us *every* detail of the ship – including the tea and coffee side of things."

John chuckled: "It's all right Ben, Collington's young and doesn't understand how boring he can be."

"I hope Dr Macintyre doesn't befriend him," said Benedict. "You know what young minds are like: they are easily influenced by stupidity."

"I know, Ben; I remember when I was a boy: there was so much influence – much more than we have now. God, I was distracted so much – it was hard to avoid it. You're right in what you said, Ben: fuckers like Dr Macintyre easily divert other young men."

"So I guess I ain't going to be able to do anything about this, am I?"

The *Levitator* had gone now, its enchanting silhouette had most likely returned to port.

"You'll be going on that thing in a few days, good luck Ben – I mean it."

Again the nervousness returned to him: he'd be far away from home, very far away from the comforts of his little community.

"I'm scared 'bout this mission, John," said Commander Nettlefold. "Shit, in all of my military career I've never been so nervous; I don't know why. It's just I haven't been given a clear role in the mission – and I haven't heard much about this 'energy' they're investigating; it's like some sort of top-secret project they're working on; as far as I know, there's only one physicist and two detectives coming, why? I mean, fucking hell, John; don't they see no sense?"

"Yeah, Ben; I mean, you'd think if it *was* a scientific mission, they would have a large team of physicists around with them; as you said, Benedict, they've more soldiers than physicists."

The two men talked late into the night, Benedict delivering the points, John backing them up. One could say that their conversation was never-ending, but there wasn't time for relaxation now; not in *this* century.

Not in this godforsaken century.

John left just after midnight; Benedict watched the glowing bus disappear round the bend, lighting up the space around it.

"Damn cold," he muttered, noticing the sudden chill. "Come on, old boy, get yourself inside where it's nice an' warm."

Two days later, Benedict was awoken by a loud knocking on his door.

Sighing, he turned to his clock and realised that he was late for Collington. He showered and dressed quickly, making sure his gun was securely in his holster. He made his way to the front door, taking his bag with him.

He didn't even glimpse the young officer, until he had put his front door keys in a special place under the patio, which he covered securely.

"Good morning, Commander," said Collington, his hat held under his arm – Benedict could see that, even in the morning darkness.

"Mornin'."

"If you'll follow me, sir, I'll show you to the car…"

"Certainly." Benedict followed Commander Collington to the track in front of his cottage. "Where's the car?" he inquired.

"It's over here." Collington let Nettlefold to a small passing place by the track; a small, brown car stood there; there was no driver sitting in it, only two empty seats.

"Is this your car?" gasped Benedict, seeing the pull-back wheel – similar to John's bus controls, and the dirty brown roof.

"No," said Commander Collington. "Mickson thought I required something much less conspicuous; this seemed perfect." He opened the door for Benedict who sat inside rather unsurely at this 'generous' behaviour from Collington.

The young commander soon sat himself as well and started the engine. Soon they were away down the country path, and into the villages.

"How long's the journey?" asked Benedict.

"About an hour."

"Should've lightened up by then."

"I hope so, Ben."

"Excuse me!" barked Commander Nettlefold suddenly. "Don't you dare call me that again!"

"I'm sorry – I thought Ben was short for Benedict."

"I mean it!" snapped Nettlefold. "I mean every fucking word of it! Don't ever! Understood?!"

"I apologise, Commander Nettlefold." Suddenly he cried: "Look out!"

A rock sailed past the front windscreen, making a dull thud with the earth on the other side of the road.

Commander Collington pushed the wheel forward, stopping the car.

"Why've you done that, Commander?" shouted Benedict, taking out his pistol. "Now we'll have to answer to them! Take your gun out, Collington."

The young officer removed his pistol and both got out the car. They soon saw what had caused the trouble: four youths armed with metal rods stood in the village green.

"Oh shit," muttered Benedict, "not these guys again!"

"Alright, pal?" one of them jeered – he had his rod pointed forward, as if casting a spell.

"Hello Rob," said Nettlefold. "What d'ya want now?"

"You still owe us a beating-up; when are we gonna get it?"

"You're not," snarled Commander Collington.

Rob shouted back: "Shut it, ya fuckin' tosser!"

Collington fired a shot; it sailed past Rob and hit the pavement.

The youths backed off, allowing them to get back into the car. As Commander Collington drove them away, they heard profanity behind them.

"That was pretty stupid!" yelled Commander Nettlefold once they'd left the village. "What in God's name were you thinking?"

"I defended us," replied the commander calmly.

Silence befell the rest of the journey.

The cold sun was bright by the time they reached the city. Commander Collington, not used to the drawback steering wheel, had great difficulty navigating round the corners.

They passed several spice markets, eventually arriving at the airport. There were trucks full of supplies being loaded onto conveyer belts. Nettlefold used them to trace the whereabouts of the ship – and there it was:

She was a stunning beauty against the morning sky, her fins singing with the wind. The *Levitator* was sat on some kind of rail that stretched to the end on the runway, her lower deck placed neatly into the groove. Guards helped load the crates into the hold, their rough hands not even stopping.

On the top deck, members of the crew watched the busy ground below, but not forgetting that they were on one of the prototype ships of the future.

If Lady Joanne could see this now…

Benedict Nettlefold got out of the car, rubbing his hands. He glimpsed General Mickson discussing something with the Minuet who was nodding in agreement.

Commander Collington signalled to a driver to take away the car, and then went to join his friends. Benedict was left alone.

"If somebody could please tell me where to go!" shouted an annoyed voice behind him.

Nettlefold turned around to face and elderly professor carrying two cases and a coat over his arm looking most confused. He wore a white, feathery jacket with a blue neckerchief tied in a loose knot round his bronze shirt. He trudged nervously in his beige shoes and trousers. This was the kind of person that Benedict respected.

"Hello sir," greeted Nettlefold, "the leaders are over there." He gestured towards the small group.

"Thank you, sir," replied the professor. "I don't believe we've met."

"I'm Commander Benedict Nettlefold, sir."

"Professor Samuel Bentley – pleased to meet you." Bentley shook hands with the commander. "Now, I believe we must go and meet our friends."

They wandered slowly over to the rich gentlemen, all of whom were now a nodding puppet show.

"Gentlemen," said Commander Nettlefold, "sir, I would like you to meet the professor – "

"We know," snapped the Minuet. "That's why we recruited him – good to meet you, sir!" He shook hands with Bentley.

As the elderly physicist greeted the other leaders, Benedict could think of nothing but hatred towards the Minuet – that stupid middle-aged piece of royalty with the same name as a dance; the Minuet's balding head shone in the morning sun and his brown eyes kept twitching towards Nettlefold – what a posh bastard; how dare he humiliate him? Just because he was royalty didn't mean he could embarrass at will; that was Dr Macintyre's job.

Nettlefold glimpsed a member of the crew approaching them – he too had a balding head, but wore a decently tidy black uniform. He had polished, gold spectacles with narrow lenses. "Gentlemen!" he cried approaching them. "Good day to all!"

"Dr Bentley," said General Mickson, "Commander Nettlefold, this is Captain Jonas Sender, commanding officer of the *Levitator*. Captain, this is Professor Samuel Bentley and this - "

"No need to introduce me to him!" smiled Captain Sender. "Commander Benedict Nettlefold, the Flag of Dedication!" He placed a fat hand on Benedict's shoulder. "This man has been on the front line of conflict, my good men; he's been out there."

"So have I," whispered General Mickson.

"I don't know you," said Nettlefold.

"No you don't, Commander. But I know you! Whilst you were fighting on the ground, I fought in zeppelins above you! I've heard about your heroic deeds, commander; we need you on this mission, trust me."

"So, we going on-board?" Commander Collington asked impatiently.

"You are an eager young man!" said Sender. "Firstly, however, we are awaiting the final members of the crew. Tame and Bristol phoned me before; said they'd be here any minute now. I don't know where Dr Macintyre is though…"

"He's onboard already, settling into his quarters I suppose," said Mickson. "Hold on, I think that's them…"

Two detectives approached them. They wore the traditional grey uniforms that all investigators wore. One of them was a man in his late forties with deep brown hair and a clip-on tie. But the other was a young woman of about twenty; she had faintly purple-coloured hair and wore a bandana around her neck. She beamed at Benedict.

General Mickson gestured towards them: "For those of you that don't know, this is Chief Inspector Albert Tame, and this here," he continued, pointing towards the young woman, "is Chief Inspector Rachel Bristol – it's her debut mission."

"Okay folks," said Captain Sender, "let's head onto the sweetheart herself."

The *Levitator* had this main central corridor that ran the length of the ship; Captain Sender introduced the non-government people to this with great pride in his voice – yes, it *was* the pride.

Bristol seemed interested in the whole thing, but kept flashing her eyes repeatedly at Benedict Nettlefold, who didn't notice it at first, but when he did, he beamed back at her.

Captain Sender gave them a full tour of the ship. When they reached the galley, he asked: "Where is Dr Macintyre? – Where *is* he?"

Finally, they reached the cockpit. All had some job getting in there due to the cramping of equipment and controls.

General Mickson sighed: "I've got to oversee a few things; come with me, Minuet."

"Of course." They both vanished into the maze below.

Chief Inspector Tame whispered something briefly to Bristol and then, eager to escape these dratted confines, he left the cockpit.

Professor Bentley stayed with them. "I can sort out my bags later," he said, "but this might be the only chance I get to see the piloting controls; you see, I've heard so much about - "

"Calm yourself, professor," said one of the pilots, "these controls are much harder than you think." He indicated the massive stick between the two seats: "You see this: this allows you to adjust the engine every thousand feet; did you know that you constantly have to move it during ascension and descending? But sometimes in stormy weather, you have to 'half adjust' the stick. Also because of the rotation of the particle emitter, you have to constantly adjust it when turning; yes, this machine is almost impossible to fly, right Barry?"

"Yeah, sure it is, Don."

Suddenly, someone stormed onto the piloting deck, stuttering angrily: "If I don't get everyone's medical reports before the mission starts, I'm afraid we might not be able to go – "

Benedict could only stare in hatred at the man, for this was the doctor who had ruined his career, his marriage, his life. He had highlighted blond hair and a blue jacket together with a tank top and red tie. He only noticed Nettlefold, because the commander had his hand on his gun. Emblazoned on his chest was a neat little badge that read:

Dr Philip Macintyre.

"Ah," said Dr Macintyre, gazing deeply at his 'patient', "I see old friends can't stop running into each other, can they?"

"You ain't a friend," snarled Benedict, "you're more like - "

"I suggest you stop, Mr Nettlefold," said Dr Macintyre, "or I'm afraid that I shall have to have you placed under arrest for insubordination; now you don't want that, do you?"

"No *sir*," replied Benedict calmly.

"Now, go to your quarters immediately," snarled Macintyre, handing Benedict a set of keys.

"Yes sir." Benedict turned to go –

"Salute me!"

"Sir." Nettlefold stiffly saluted and marched out of the cockpit. He tore himself down the corridor, hearing the doctor and Captain Sender laugh at him.

Miraculously, Benedict managed to find his quarters. They were located near the bottom of the ship, amongst the hustle and bustle of the many military men coming with them. Nettlefold opened the door and slammed it behind him.

"Shit, fuckin' cunt!" he yelled as he threw himself down onto his bed. "How fucking dare he!"

The door opened and someone came in – Bristol. She'd followed Benedict from the cockpit.

"I thought I'd shut that door," muttered Nettlefold.

"No you didn't," she replied. "You should take more care, Commander."

"Look, sweetheart," he whispered, "are you on my side – or his?"

"Commander, I came to make sure you were all right, that's all."

"Oh, I get it, detective: I'm supposed to go cryin' into your arms, bursting my fuckin' tears out – then you use that as an excuse to tell Dr Macintyre that I'm a weak fucking cunt, and then he uses *that* as an excuse to fuckin' sue me."

"Commander, I'm not that sorta person, alright? I just wanted to make sure everything was okay, alright?"

"Then shut the door."

Bristol clicked it shut.

"Listen," she said, "I don't think we've been properly introduced to each other. I'm Rachel Bristol," she announced.

"Commander Benedict Nettlefold," replied the stubborn person before her.

"I heard what happened to you, Commander – Dr Macintyre did something terrible to you, didn't he? He made up a rumour about you, and ruined your wedding."

"He did something more awful than that, Miss Bristol – he fucked up my career as well; everything I had, he fucking ruined."

"You know he's getting married?"

Nettlefold sneered. "Who to? Some poor bitch in Madagascar?"

Bristol chuckled slightly; "No, not to her – no, he's getting married to a woman called Adeline Paulington."

"What?!" vociferated Benedict. "Right, that's fuckin' it!" He reached inside his coat and pulled out his gun. "I'm going to kill that cunt once and for all! By fucking God, I want his shit spread throughout his motherfucking grave!"

Nettlefold snatched several more bullets from his pocket and filled every hole in the barrel. "Then once I've killed him, I'm going' to shoot him again, until he's dead for fuckin' sure!"

"Commander, please!" Bristol cried. "Come on, you know what he'll do if you go for him... Please stop, Benedict."

Suddenly Benedict was overcome with burning nervousness; the gun slackened deeply in his hands and his mouth twisted with sheer weakness. "Fuck," he muttered quietly to himself, then to Bristol: "Jesus fuckin' Christ, I'm sorry; guess, I ain't that great any more, am I?"

"You're only eighteen," the detective replied.

"So I keep being reminded; fuck, I guess I'm gonna have to recognise *exactly* who I am."

"You feel better now?" Bristol inquired.

"Yeah." But the anger soon returned: "Now, Miss Bristol, tell Dr Macintyre that if he comes near me again, I'll blow his fuckin' brains out, alright? No," he whispered sarcastically, "we don't want to upset the good doctor, do we?"

About an hour later, the *Levitator* was high up in the sky.

Benedict had received permission to go into the piloting deck and watch the two skilled men pilot the machine through the clouds; the guy called Don, who was the main pilot, seemed as if to be playing an instrument the way he constantly moved the stick back and forth, changing the engine setting.

Benedict just couldn't believe how they did it:

Whenever the engine reached an optimum level, a red light on the dashboard seemed to glow. The pilot then seemed to grasp the stick, pull in some kind of lever on it, and move it to another position.

But then when they entered a wind current, the setting had to change – so the pilots would then grasp this stick, but instead of pulling the lever back completely, they half pulled it.

Benedict was lost as to how they did it.

But the *Levitator* glided on, occasionally passing a zeppelin or a balloon. There was little activity on them now: everything was much too silent at this time of day.

They passed over Essex, seeing the small rural villages and towns, bathing in the light. Captain Sender informed them that this was the last they'd ever see of England.

Suddenly, Don pulled back the wheel and adjusted the stick. They advanced up into the clouds, the wind rattling the framework outside.

Benedict fancied staying in with the pilots and Sender, watching the sky and other ships – but then Dr Macintyre came in.

Chapter 4   Attack

Late into the evening, the *Levitator* passed over the Ural Mountains.

As Benedict sat in his chair in the lounge gazing at the wonders below, he couldn't help but think of something: his future; what would become of him once this mission was over? Would he return home and retire? Would he stay in the military and try serving his career a little higher up in the league of things? Many choices – but each one, each single one was something for Dr Macintyre to investigate.

This wasn't his first mission though; he'd been on many throughout him seemingly long but short military career – many adventures indeed.

But times had long since changed.

In the old days, there was good old classic adventure – in the days of Lady Joanne. Yes, a classical adventure story: a man would be become part of an expedition to reach out into the unknown – on the expedition would be the brave senior leader, the beautiful girl, the cantankerous professor, a few other men and the convoy of cars, trucks and planes used to explore the foreign land.

But times had long since changed.

Now the only expeditions of exploration were to small mountain tops, ice and unreachable valleys that were deemed a threat to civilisation. It would normally comprise of a series of state-of-the-art machinery, lots and lots of guns, zeppelins – basically just like the old days, only more advanced. But there was one main difference: some distance away from the expedition destination there would be a launcher equipped with several fourteen megaton nuclear missiles that could be fired at the mountain top, or the ice, or the unreachable valley at a Moments notice. This was set up by the Epsilon Force as a means to ensure security should the expedition find any 'nasty threats'. Entire lost civilisations could be wiped out with this method.

No one could take any chances anymore.

Benedict glimpsed that doctor sitting with the command crew, drinking a gin and tonic, laughing so loudly – at him. The medic wasn't drunk, no good men never got drunk: they had to be on the constant watch out, making sure no one had too much goodness in their life.

Dr Macintyre was the kind of guy who hated good working folk, but he had this aura about him that *made* you, if you were rich and had power, to sit down with him and drink champagne 24/7.

Yeah fuckin' right I'd want to sit down with him – I've got better things to do than sit down with a right fuckin' –

As Nettlefold sat back in the couch, he realised that Dr Macintyre was making remarks about him:

"Did you hear about this Commander Benedict Nettlefold – what a stupid idiot! What a stupid name, too! Sounds like something you get from, I dunno, a landfill site!"

General Mickson and the Minuet burst out laughing. Even Commander Collington sniggered a little – obviously he needed a good laugh. Captain Sender was in hysterics – even though the joke wasn't actually particularly funny, it created a social atmosphere, and in this day and age, one needed it.

Some of the other officers and crew were approaching the senior staff to listen to Macintyre's next joke. Very soon, the entire lounge was gathered around the doctor, listening intently and laughing when even his name was mentioned.

Benedict, the sad and lonely guy he was, stood up slowly and trudged out of the lounge, making his way down the long, monotonous corridor. Perhaps that cobra colada had made his head spin: had he imagined it? No, you cannot imagine Dr Macintyre's insults, for they ruined many a man, cutting through the social societies like sharp discs, finally finding an unfortunate victim, and then ripping him up like paper.

A few crew and officers who were on night duty passed him – occasionally they nodded at him; Benedict waved back, but he was too tired and weak for any long conversations. Glancing at his watch he realised it was late.

As Commander Nettlefold approached his quarters, a young man, a steward, came up to him.

"Commander," he said, "I need to talk to you about something – my name's Bradley and I want you to know that I perfectly agree with you about Dr Macintyre – I know, he's a right bastard, but you haven't a clue of what he's really capable of."

"Let me guess, fucking other people's cunts."

"More or less – he has the power to destroy your bank account, your home, your dreams, even – "

"You should have informed me about this earlier," said Benedict. "Then I'd have fucked him first."

"He's ex-Omegan."

"What?!"

"I told ya – he's ex-Omegan; the Omega Brotherhood, he used to be a part of it."

"You'd better come in," said the commander, opening his door. Inside, the steward could find no place to sit, but was glad when Benedict Nettlefold pulled out a chair from under the bed.

"Dr Macintyre used to serve the Omega guys many years ago," Bradley implied. "Now, although he serves them no longer, he still thinks like one."

"What's the danger of that? He's destroyed me already."

"Commander Nettlefold, he *knows* everything about you."

"Which implies?"

"He's got tactics, Mr Nettlefold – if you slag him off, he'll bloody well kill you!"

Benedict seemed puzzled at the steward's somewhat strange behaviour. Quietly, he asked: "What exactly d'you want from me?"

"Nothing," replied Bradley. "Just stay here while I find out information about him."

"And how do you intend to do that – he's got tactics, remember?"

"I intend to sneak into his quarters later tonight – and pinch his diary; I'll take a look into it and see what he's got planned."

Benedict sat down, hissing. "Why do you want *me* to know this?"

"I just need you to stay out of the way."

"I was victimised by that cunt, thank you very much, Mr Bradley. Now if you're going after this stupid, thick individual, I want to come, so I can take some of his stuff."

"That's the danger, Benedict: you want to hurt him. If you let your personal feelings get in the way of things, I might fail in my task – but I'll make sure you know exactly what's in the diary."

"Okay," said Benedict, shrugging in a sarcastic manner. "If you want to go fuck yourself, then do it. Without my help, you'll fail – and Dr Macintyre will probably have you strung up."

"Alright; wish me luck then."

"Good luck."

Suddenly, there was a silence. Then a massive crash. The entire *Levitator* seemed to shake with thunderous applause.

In the lounge, Captain Sender heard this too.

He dropped his glass, and then threw himself to his feet, taking out his pistol. "Everyone, stay here!" he barked; then, beckoning to General Mickson, Commander Collington, Dr Macintyre and the irascible Minuet, he summoned them out of the common room, dashing past the bartender.

Dr Macintyre drew his pistol, making sure that it was at the ready. Commander Collington seemed too nervous to even check his gun was loaded at all.

Suddenly, a servant came dashing at them. "Sirs!" he cried. "Oh please, sirs! Please! There're some pirates I think back there!"

"Calm yourself, my dear man!" shouted Dr Macintyre. "Now, my dear fellow, tell us where these gentlemen are, then maybe we can hunt them down."

"There in the central promenade." The servant seemed obviously too scared to continue, but nevertheless gestured once more in the direction of the attackers, and dashed off.

They crept along, silently, but in a hurry, for pirates didn't care whether they blew the ship to pieces – just as long as they got the booty.

The four pirates had based a firing ring in the main section of the central promenade. The sight of them made everyone in sight cringe. There were three males and one tall ugly female. All four of them were young, around twenty, and dressed from head to foot in black leather. Each of them carried a thick steel sabre and a variety of sore-looking blades.

The commanding staff had set themselves in firing positions, behind several crates, with a good deal of security behind them. Collington had now drawn his pistol and had just finished loading it, when Dr Macintyre called out:

"You're not welcome here! Get off this ship at once! D'you hear me? Get your souls off this ship, or else we'll fire upon you – now you don't want that do you?"

One of the pirates, the female with steel rings cut into her black skin, trudged forward, her scaly boots dragging on the floor.

"Where's ya captain?" she enquired in a raspy little voice, sounding deeply like African. "Tell me motherfuckers, where's ya fuckin' captain?"

"I'm here," said Sender bravely, walking forward. "What d'you want from us? We are on a mission to investigate attacks in Pacifica – we do not require your assistance; now get off my ship."

"Yeah, I see your ship is neat. But I don't wanna fuck it."

"How dare you speak about the *Levitator* like that!" snarled Captain Sender. "She's more beautiful like you."

"More beautiful than me?" the black woman sneered. "I'm more gorgeous, don't ya think."

"Who the hell *are* you to speak such disgraceful words?" Captain Sender shouted.

"Gorge Rail."

The entire promenade fell silent in fear, as this pirate was the most feared one in the world. Gorge Rail was merciless, crude, and struck fear into any who fought her. Over ten thousand men had been slashed up by her sabre.

But Captain Sender was never one to be told what to do. With boiling rage he whispered hoarsely: "Get off my ship or I'll put every bullet from this gun into your filthy self."

"So ya wanna have it out like that…"

Suddenly Gorge Rail flung herself in a spin at Sender and in one swift strike, swung her sabre down and cut of his legs at the kneecaps.

Captain Sender dropped down in a pool of dark blood, screaming like a newborn child, waving his arms in the air in one last plea for mercy.

But Gorge Rail's did not know mercy. She slashed down and sliced open Captain Sender's throat. Thick red stuff oozed rapidly out of his neck. Sender tried to hold it in with his hands, but without success as suddenly it bubbled through his fingers, spewing, gurgling, gargling, throwing its way through. The captain fell floor, choking and shuddering like a burst water pipe.

"No!" screamed Commander Collington in horror, watching Sender's final movements, before Gorge Rail raised her sword and struck down again and…

... severed off his head.

"Take that, you Epsilon piece of shit!" snarled Gorge Rail. "That's payment. Now, give us every thing on this ship that's worth money or else – "

She didn't have time to finish her words, for three gunshots rang out from down the promenade. Her three companions were gunned down instantly.

All turned to see Benedict Nettlefold standing further down the hall, a smoking gun in his hands. He was a dark figure in a dark world. He pulled back the hammer and said to the pirate: "Get off this ship immediately."

Gorge Rail was enraged: someone was daring to stand up to her by killing her ruthless companions. She prepared to strike him, but then suddenly he fired another shot. It hit her in the hand, causing her to drop the sabre. It clattered to the floor, breaking in two.

"You Epsilon – " she prepared to insult.

But Benedict fired a third time, catching her in the arm.

"Don't fuck around with me!" he yelled. "If you want to fuck something, then fuck something worth fucking!" He fired yet again. The bullet pierced her abdomen.

But the black woman seemed strangely unaffected by this. She reached to her belt and pulled out a sword, more like a long dagger, and in one sudden movement, threw herself at Commander Nettlefold, jumping down on him.

Benedict's gun dropped to the floor and he was pushed back very hard. Gorge Rail tried to stab him, but Benedict launched a punch into her face.

Then she kicked him back – and Benedict fell through a window, hitting the smooth outline of the ship like an eggshell. "Jesus Christ!" he snarled, struggling to grip onto the smooth metal. He panicked as the realisation of death came to him. But his hands found a small railing that ran the ship. Gripping onto it, he allowed himself to hang there.

The black pirate jumped out; one might have expected for her to fall off the edge of the ship, but pirates were generally well experienced in situations like these; she slid down completely in control and then hit the railing. Her long dagger was fully extended as she swiped at Commander Nettlefold.

"You gonna die!" she jeered, brandishing the knife dangerously close to Benedict's throat.

But the well experienced commander snatched her wrist, grabbing the knife and pointing it directly at her instead; he curled his hand around her forehead and snarled:

"Fuck this!"

But the pirate threw a second hand round the railings and kicked Benedict again, causing him to collapse slightly – but suddenly, quick as a lightening strike, the commander swung the dagger forward and cut off the her hands.

The pirate screamed as she fell off the deck, smashing into the lower hull, trying to grab something, but with no success as her handless arms slipped down the hull, leaving a trail of dark blood behind.

Benedict glanced down to see Gorge Rail fall into the void below. With disgust, he used the dagger to prod the bloody hands off the railing and then began to climb up, using the knife to grip the hull. He was suddenly aware that a cold wind was passing him; it was so cold.

Two crewmen appeared in the broken window and lowered a rope towards Nettlefold. He climbed up it and reached the aperture.

"Good job done," said one of them, helping him back into the ship.

"Just duty," replied Benedict – then he saw the crowd of officers and men before him, even Commander Collington was reaching out a hand to him.

They all saw how strong he was in defending the ship. Most of the younger crewmen thought his strength was admirable; the senior staff recognised their impaired judgements on him, for Commander Nettlefold was no rapist or murderer – he was a soldier who fought in a war, that's all he was: a soldier who defended his country.

For a moment Benedict felt the warmth of friendship shine on him. He felt pride of who he was.

But then he saw Dr Macintyre stooped over the dead body of one of the pirates, with his stethoscope on the pirate's chest and he was listening quite intently.

Commander Nettlefold was enraged. He glanced around on the floor for his pistol and, finding it, picked the weapon up and went over to Dr Macintyre.

"Get up," Benedict said menacingly as he lowered the gun to Macintyre's head. "Get up, you bastard!"

"How dare you!" shouted Dr Macintyre through gritted teeth. "I'm trying to do my job; can you not see that?"

"They're dead, Dr Macintyre," retorted Benedict. "You don't even need to be a nurse to work that out."

"They may not be," said Macintyre. "Now screw off before I have you locked in irons."

"I think I should pull this trigger and put a bullet in your head, Dr Macintyre," sneered Benedict.

"I could have you sent to prison for that," cried Macintyre, standing up. "In fact I will! I know one of the best prosecution lawyers in the world – and he'll have you sent to prison for many years, perhaps life! Security, detain this man below decks."

"Wait just a minute," said Benedict Nettlefold as security guards approached him. He opened the gun and held it up for everyone to see. "No bullets in it," he announced. "Now, Dr Macintyre, I'm not a lawyer, but doesn't the law state something like this:

"The law cannot arrest anyone threatening another with a gun if the gun is unloaded or is loaded with blanks?"

"It's true," said one of the guards.

"Now, Dr Macintyre, if you will excuse me, I would like to return to my quarters and rest." Benedict began to trudge out of the promenade, passing through the crowd that had gathered.

Miraculously, the young members of the crew still stepped forwards to shake his hand.

Knowing that he wouldn't get out of the promenade if he didn't return the favour, he agreeably smiled and appreciated the rare warmth he was receiving.

Benedict felt like a powerful leader walking through his supporters, all of whom eagerly wanting to meet him. Benedict felt a true leader, appreciating all that the rank of 'commander' could offer. He felt like he'd overlooked it – being a commander wasn't that bad at times.

Right now it felt like heaven.

But as he passed through the last members of the crowd, General Mickson reached out his hand and he shook it accordingly.

It was what he saw in the general's eyes that shocked Benedict deeply. For it was not a congratulating look, nor a look of admiration, not even a look of hatred or jealousy but a look of a deeply concealed fear.

Chapter 5   Assault on Pacifica

Captain Sender's loss shattered the crew.

Some of the very young crewmembers demanded to return home and, after careful consideration among themselves, set up a miniature protest in the promenade.

The senior staff took notice of them and retired to a small room just below the piloting deck and debated it for several hours. An overall decision was reached: return home.

But then they received a transmission from King Christopher ordering them to continue with the mission; Sender's first officer, Lieutenant Bilston, was to be put in charge of the ship.

Professor Bentley was horrified at what had happened to Captain Sender, as any old-fashioned professor was inclined to do on an old-fashioned expedition. But these were new times – the professor was repeatedly informed by General Mickson that Sender had challenged a feared pirate and had suffered by her hand.

It didn't matter to Commander Nettlefold: he spent the majority of the time in his quarters as there was nothing much for him to do. Even the scenery outside wasn't interesting: just a blue expanse above and a blue expanse below.

When he wasn't couched up in his quarters, he often spent time talking with the pilots about how they operated the incredibly complex machine; there seemed to be no end to the random patterns of the switches and levers.

You could put God in the piloting seat and even He wouldn't know how to fly it.

Dr Macintyre was still cursing silently at Benedict out the corner of his mouth. Benedict felt pride at what he'd done to the doctor. His worst enemy had learnt his lesson.

But this pride was short-lived.

The day after King Christopher's transmission, Dr Macintyre banned Commander Nettlefold from carrying a loaded pistol. The servant Bradley had protested against this – but a servant was a mere sand grain compared to Macintyre. He had the servant confined to quarters.

Commander Collington had also made a protest at Nettlefold's 'punishment for defiance', much to both Macintyre's and Benedict's surprise. He said that the commander should – for ship's security – have a loaded pistol on him at all times.

But Dr Macintyre merely ignored him.

Detective Bristol was furious at this as well. She made multiple complaints to Macintyre and General Mickson to have the ban removed.

Again Dr Macintyre displayed ignorance: not even General Mickson could tell him to stop 'treating' his patients.

However, word was soon sent to King Christopher who immediately came to Commander Nettlefold's defence, saying that under security regulations, all armed members of the Epsilon Brotherhood had to have a loaded weapon on them.

After much hassle, it was decided that the commander should be allowed to keep the bullets in his pocket.

Benedict seemed slightly overjoyed at this, but soon he realised that it made little difference to his condition: Dr Macintyre had control of him, whatever the weather. A little later, he seemed too weak to show any kind of smile; all he could manage was a faint snort.

It was a week after this that the commander lay sullen in his quarters, oblivious to anything but his own thoughts.

What if he'd never met Dr Macintyre? Maybe his life would've taken a different turn. He would've been married to Adeline. But now that bastard Macintyre was marrying her.

It *was* Benedict's own fault: he'd let slip and fallen into Macintyre's hell-made grasp. His life had been ruined. He'd lost the commission he'd always dreamed of.

A knock on the door made him lower his eyes from the ceiling. "Yeah, who is it?" he asked out loud.

"It's me, Chief Inspector Tame."

"Come in."

The ageing detective stumbled into Nettlefold's quarters, brushing his thin, streaky hair to the side with his hand. He'd heard about Commander Nettlefold once, two years ago: something to do with a heroic act of preventing genocide – but that *was* two years ago; now Benedict was someone else – he had changed from fearless to fearsome.

And that made Tame petrified of what he had to do next.

But he was relieved when the commander interjected: "How long until we reach Pacifica?"

"A week at most," replied the detective. "The pilots are working twice as fast, but even so it'll take some time to get there."

"What did you come here for?"

"I got sent here." Chief Inspector Tame was now obviously scared; his fingers trembled and his knees buckled slightly.

"Who sent you?"

"That doesn't matter – I just need to check if your pistol is loaded for security."

Benedict was enraged. "Alright," he snarled, "where is he?"

"I shouldn't speak his whereabouts."

Tame backed away from Commander Nettlefold, making sure he could get away out the door in a flash second should he need to. The elderly detective just couldn't sum up the strength to carry out Macintyre's orders. However, he shut his eyes briefly and, keeping them closed, said: "Commander, what I'm about to say isn't of my own making, but comes directly from Dr Macintyre. Please do not feel rage due to these orders."

"What the hell does he want?"

"As well as wanting me to check your pistol," Tame stuttered, "he wants… he wants…"

"Spit it out!"

"He wants me… to remove the firing plug from your gun."

"You can tell him that I do not wish to have it removed," replied Benedict with faked politeness.

"He says once we get to Pacifica, you can have it back."

"Like hell," said Benedict. "Who does that fucker think he is? The king himself?"

"Let's not be gruff," whispered Chief Inspector Tame nervously. "Just give me the firing plug."

"Alright, my weapon carries no bullets." Benedict took out his gun and opened it, showing Tame that it was indeed unloaded.

"The firing plug please…"

"Here it is." Benedict reached into the gun and removed the minuscule piece of metal, the stuff that enabled the gun to fire. When the gun was fired, the hammer struck the firing plug, creating a small electrical charge. Inside the bullet at the back was a small section of aerated water, and at the back of the bullet was a microscopic package of rubidium sealed tightly. The electrical charge struck the bullet, causing the package of rubidium to burst; the rubidium reacted with the water, creating a fiery explosion that set off the gunpowder. The bullet then shot out the end and struck the unlucky victim at the other.

But now that the metal firing plug had been removed, there was no chance of that happening.

"Thank you," replied Tame, putting the plug in his pocket. "Now that the gun will not fire, you may keep it loaded." Tame paused for a few seconds. "If there are no other questions or comments…"

"Yes, one: why do you continue to serve that selfish brat? You know what he does is wrong…"

"Wait a minute, Commander," said Tame, raising his left hand. "You are quite wrong when you say that, for Dr Macintyre would *never* do anything out of line. He is a young, ambitious doctor, but he isn't the sort of person you have just described him as. Macintyre's a gentleman."

"No he's not!" barked Benedict. "He is a complete shithead, that's what he is!"

"That was very impolite – "

"It's bleeding fact!"

"Okay," said Tame quietly, "that's enough. That's quite enough. Dr Macintyre's just down the corridor seeing to an airsick soldier. I'm getting him in here right now."

Tame vanished out the door.

"Shit," muttered Benedict. "Macintyre's gonna have me arrested, and I don't have a God damn gun on me that works."

Benedict panicked: how could he escape from these quarters? He searched around frantically for a place to hide, but then, hearing the trampling of feet coming down the corridor, he had an idea.

Suddenly, Macintyre, Tame and three guards entered the cabin.

"Sit down on the bed, Mr Nettlefold," ordered Dr Macintyre, watching as the commander slowly lowered himself onto the mattress. "Now, slowly hand over your pistol."

Benedict raised the gun by the barrel, but suddenly he let it slip from his hand. It fell off the mattress and dropped into the cavity between the bed and the wall.

"Pick it up," sneered Macintyre, "you useless, inferior serviceman."

Benedict twisted over, lying flat on the bed, reaching down into the space. There he saw exactly what he wanted: the lowest bed railing had been done in a pattern that had the metal divided into a spiral. The railing was made of the same material as the firing plug.

"It's a little stuck down here," he announced. "It'll take a minute to dislodge it. It's caught in a small hole in the floor."

This bought him the time he needed to carefully snap off a tiny piece of the railing. He picked up the pistol from where it lay and, quick as a flash, slid the metal into the slot.

He slowly raised himself from the mattress, feeling nauseated as the blood drained from his head.

"You know what's going to happen, don't you?" laughed Macintyre. "You'll be taken from here down to the cells." Then he laughed even more. "No, you won't be. Guards, I want you to kill this pest with his own gun. Make it look like he shot himself."

"Should we be doing this?" Chief Inspector Tame asked in shock. "He hasn't committed a huge crime, sir, he's only made a cheeky comment about you."

"Too many," said Macintyre. "Let's go." He followed Tame out of the cabin, smiling victoriously at Benedict.

The three guards cornered the commander by the bed. One of them reached out his hand to grab Benedict's gun.

Suddenly, the commander fired the gun at the guard's palm.

"Fuck!" cried the injured security guard as the toxin in the bullet began dissolving his fingers. They dropped off like apples from a tree, padding the carpet with a red-green soup of rotting flesh. "Fuck! Holy fucking fuck!"

The guard dropped to the floor, trying hopelessly to stop the toxin spreading.

The other two guards began closing in on Benedict. He suddenly whipped round and fired the gun again, but the nothing happened: the bed railing must have fallen out.

"Grab him," said the third guard.

Benedict was seized by the second guard.

"Take this!" cried the third guard removing a blade.

But Benedict kicked the guard's hand, causing the sword to pierce straight through his throat. There was a sudden squelching as an artery was severed open. Blood spat out and cried furiously down his uniform.

"Take that, you bastard!" yelled Benedict, elbowing the guard restraining him. He yanked out his gun with such force that the guard stumbled rearwards.

Benedict used this opportunity to aim the gun and plunged five bullets into the second guard. "Take that," he said defiantly.

Suddenly from behind him, there was the sound of a blade being lifted up. His heart nearly stopped when he turned round to see the partially dissolved guard raise the sword. Half of his face was clinging to his skull by a thread as his right arm bled furiously.

Benedict threw himself at the guard, flinging him over his head. The guard smashed threw the window, shrieking like a banshee as he fell into the clouds.

He threw away the pistol and picked up his own. He needed to find Tame to retrieve the firing plug. In the meantime, a piece of bed frame would have to suffice. He plucked another bit off and shoved it into his gun.

The corridor was empty as he ran down it. Everyone must have been having lunch. That meant Dr Macintyre was probably in the lounge dining with the senior officers.

Benedict felt a dull pain in his side. His first thought was that a stray bullet had caught him in his hip, but as he opened his jacket, he noticed that his voice recorder had penetrated through the lining and dug into his shirt.

He cracked a smile when he realised that the recorder had been accidentally switched on. He could use this to bring down Macintyre! But not in front of the *Levitator* crew, for they would destroy the tape in a second – but in front of King Christopher. The king was prone to siding with Macintyre, but should he hear the recording, perhaps His Majesty would use his powers to destroy Macintyre's career.

Benedict darted back to his quarters and locked the tape away securely. Shutting the door behind him and turning the key, he made his way to the lounge.

He had just turned a corner two corridors away from there, when someone came jogging after him. At first he thought it was Dr Macintyre wanting to put an end to him once and for all, but instead he found himself confronted by Lieutenant Bilston.

"Commander!" said Bilston breathlessly.

"What is it, sir?"

"You're needed in the meeting room immediately! Mickson's there already – we've just received news about the Omegans!"

Benedict followed the lieutenant to the meeting room. Security guards and officers were dotted around outside. Bilston pushed his way through followed by Commander Nettlefold.

Benedict hated crowds, and he could feel the heat radiating off all of the stressed bodies around him. He was frightened that he would suddenly be crushed like a nut if everyone fell on top of him.

They ploughed through the crowd, Bilston shouting, "Commanding Officer!" Gradually they made their way through the confused mass and into the chamber itself.

The huge oval table was rapidly being cleaned and the water glasses being filled. General Mickson was sitting at the head with Commander Collington and Dr Macintyre sitting on either side of him. Professor Bentley, Tame, Bristol and the Minuet entered and searched the nameplates for where they were due to sit.

Lieutenant Bilston took his seat, leaving Benedict to search for his seat himself. He soon found it: a chair next to Bristol with a desk nameplate engraved harshly with the words *Commander Benedict Nettlefold*.

Dr Macintyre and Tame saw him both at the same time and both, particularly the medic, flashed hatred and fear at him.

Other crewmembers began filling the oval table; those that did not have an allocated seat stood to the side, crowded together like chickens waiting for the slaughter.

Nevertheless, soon the room was filled and everyone waited for General Mickson to speak.

The senior general remained seated as he took out several reports, placed them on the desk and then put his hands in a steeple.

"Ladies and gentlemen," he said hesitantly, "three hours ago, the Omega Brotherhood attacked our one and only colony in Pacifica: the seaside town of Port Dickens. The local security had no chance as the Omegans moved through butchering all who lay in their path. No prisoners were taken, and only a handful of people escaped. They managed to escape from the island in a raft and were rescued by a fishing boat later.

"As far as we know, Port Dickens itself has been left unharmed, but some of our crafts have seen the Omegans putting artillery weapons into the streets. The beach itself is being fitted with weapons that will massacre anyone who tries to get in by sea. The crafts have also spotted some kind of missile launcher in the main town square.

"King Christopher has sent a transmission ordering us to take out the launcher and free the town. We can't enter by land, because there are too many patrols; we can't enter by sea due to the guns on the beach. Our only option is to parachute in, land on the beach and fight our way to the town square."

"Why not just parachute directly into the square itself or launch rockets at it from the *Levitator*?" Benedict asked.

"We can't parachute into the square," informed General Mickson, "because of the skyward pointing rocket launchers in there and we can't destroy the missile, because it contains a very dangerous weapon."

"What kind of weapon, general?" someone from the audience asked.

But suddenly there was an uproar of noise as other crewmembers made inquiries and Mickson pretended not to hear. The general signalled to Commander Collington.

Collington stood up and made sure he had everyone's attention before he spoke. "Er, folks, I know this is a deviation from our original plan of settling down in Pacifica quietly, however, once we've secured Port Dickens, we will regroup on the *Levitator*. Then we will continue the mission."

Benedict couldn't believe Collington's words! He didn't have a clue what he was talking about! 'Stuttering' was what they called it back at the academy.

Benedict stood up, surprising the audience. "Ladies and gentlemen!" he called loudly. "Ladies and gentlemen!" he shouted again, silencing the chamber. "Commander Collington is incapable of delivering a solid speech on the matter. Would someone who knows clearly of this matter and can speak without this 'stutter' please rise up and talk."

"Commander Nettlefold, please sit down," General Mickson ordered quietly.

"Just a moment, general – "

"Sit down!" Dr Macintyre barked loudly. "Now!"

Grudgingly, Benedict lowered himself back down onto his seat; he didn't dare argue with Macintyre about anything, for the medic would have him removed of his gun altogether.

General Mickson motioned for Collington to carry on. The young officer glared angrily at Benedict before he continued his speech.

"As I was saying, we hope to carry on with the mission as normal the second Port Dickens is secure; only some people shall require to stay there and guard it while we complete the objectives of the mission. His Majesty has stated just that…"

"Fucking prick," Benedict whispered to himself as Commander Collington finished speaking and gestured towards the senior general.

"Thank you, commander; now, the king has given me specifications on the actual attack." Mickson paused as he glanced down at the paper in front of him. "He has stated that every soldier in the Epsilon Force will join the attack, along with the guards, save those ones guarding important sections of the *Levitator* – I will further specify which guards join the attack later. He wants a quarter of the attacking guards to remain in Port Dickson once the attack is over. Our initial plan to stop at the Edge of Asia before we make the final leap to Pacifica is hereby cancelled. We intend to strike directly at the seaside port. The pilots will soon put the *Levitator* up to maximum velocity and we should reach Pacifica by tomorrow morning. Once there, we will parachute at 08:00 hours."

"Thank you, General Mickson," said Dr Macintyre, standing up. "You are all to return to your quarters and prepare yourselves for tomorrow. All those selected for the attack meet in the Drop Room at 07:30 hours sharp. Anything else, general…"

"Just one thing: as I said before, I will specify which guards are required for the attack. If you are selected, expect a notice through your door within the next hour. That is all – crew dismissed."

The crowd began to file out, a seething mass of stressed out people living in this hard bent world. Nevertheless, Benedict used this to inch his way towards Chief Inspector Tame who seemed to be trying to hide from the commander in the massive crowd. But the good commander found him and grabbed him by the elbow.

"The firing plug, Mr Tame," growled Benedict. "Now."

"Look – "

"I need it for tomorrow, inspector," Benedict snarled, grabbing the detective by the neck and twisting him so Tame's back was against his chest. "So give me the god damn firing plug!"

"Here it is." Tame handed over the tiny piece of metal and dashed off quickly, yelling remarks back.

Benedict opened his gun, removed the bed piece and then put the real plug into the barrel. He snapped up the weapon quickly and put it in his holster. "Cowardly arrogant son of a bitch," he accused Tame quietly.

Benedict hurried out of the chamber, narrowly missing Dr Macintyre who was about to deliver another line of restrictions. Macintyre thought about pursuing the commander to his quarters, but decided that it wasn't worth it: tomorrow they would both go into battle, side by side. The chances were that a weak fool such as Benedict would perish in the first few seconds.

Benedict couldn't sleep that night.

His thoughts kept drifting back in time many years to when he was five and heard the tales of Lady Joanne and her missions to destroy the evil in this world. There were countless stories and legends of soldiers going on these missions, plunging themselves into epic adventures in foreign lands with beautiful women, cantankerous professors, and of course, the enemy. But the enemy was always someone who openly admitted to being the enemy himself.

However, all these missions and adventures led to one thing happening: the Battle of the Vine. The legendary battle in which Lady Joanne was killed and the twenty-four brotherhoods were created. When the brotherhoods began to fall, the enemy changed. He wasn't the evil person that destroyed people in adventures; he was someone different. The enemy had become part of the world itself. Sometimes the enemy was the person everyone thought popular. And he killed not with guns, rockets or sorcery, but with words.

As Benedict thought about this, his hand reached out and picked up his gun. It would be morning soon and he wanted the gun loaded and ready before he got up. He filled up the barrel and put the gun in his coat.

He glanced at his watch: 0630 hours. He'd better get up anyway. Slowly but surely he sat up and put his head in his hands, realising that today would be his first battle in ages. Benedict reached under his bed and removed his uniform. It was old and battered as it hadn't been used for years: Nettlefold much preferred to do his home duties in civilian clothing. Not that the police much cared. As long as he had a form of identification on him when he was doing his tasks, they weren't bothered about how he dressed.

He put the dark blue uniform on, fastening up the zip and doing up any loose pockets. He sighed with annoyance when it came to the shoes: they didn't bare any ankle support whatsoever; they were just ordinary smart shoes. However, he duly put them on, and then, slotting his gun into his holster, began to make his way to the Drop Room.

Benedict was surprised when he entered, for seeing General Mickson, Dr Macintyre and Commander Collington all wearing thick leather jumpsuits startled him – he didn't expect Dr Macintyre to be going, however his true role on this mission was to provide medical support, and that meant going into the field of battle.

He was early, so none of the troops had arrived yet. Benedict cautiously approached the doctor and said: "Commander Nettlefold, signing in – sir."

Macintyre said nothing. He pointed to a jumpsuit in the corner. Benedict went over to it and began pulling it on. First his feet went into the sealed smooth sock ends of the legs, and then he pulled up the leather to his waist. There was a holster attached to the suit for his gun. Groaning, he pulled off his traditional belt and holster that was causing him some aggravation around the waist as the suit was tight. He was now able to clip the waist belt of the jumpsuit tightly. Benedict pulled up the suit and clipped it around the neck.

"Here." General Mickson handed him a pair of gloves and some boots. "You can put your holster back in your quarters."

Benedict fitted on the gloves that clamped harshly on his wrists, and then turned his attention to the boots. They were thick and hard to get on, as he was already wearing shoes covered in the leather socks of the jumpsuit. Nevertheless, everyone had to do this, so he shoved the left boot on first, then the right. He fastened the tall boots as tight as he could and then stood up holding his pistol. Carefully he placed it in the holster and did up the cover.

Finally finished, Benedict Nettlefold, a commander, made his way over to the group.

Mickson ran his hand through his ginger hair and moustache and gazed at the commander. "You can put your traditional holster back in your cabin now, Commander."

"Yes sir," replied Benedict. He dashed back to his room and put the holster in a cupboard. Sighing to himself, he retraced his steps to the Drop Room.

Other soldiers and the selected guards had arrived and had begun to don their parachutes. No masks were required as the drop was from a low altitude.

It was nearing 08:00 hours and General Mickson kept glancing at his watch nervously. Dr Macintyre also seemed keen to get this over and done with.

A soldier handed Benedict his parachute and the commander clipped the small pack on. Commander Nettlefold chewed his teeth nervously, for he had never done a drop before, and this first drop was into battle. He felt like vomiting, but contained the urge, for Dr Macintyre would think him weak.

Someone tapped him on the shoulder. He glanced round to see Chief Inspector Bristol standing behind him.

"I just wanted to say good luck, commander," the girl said nervously.

"Thanks," replied Commander Nettlefold. "Best of luck here as well. When I return we can share our stories."

"Alright then."

"Yeah, alright!" Both of them laughed, and then looked each other in the eye.

"I'll see you later, Rachel," he said. "Oh, shit. Crap. We're not on first-name basis. I'll try that again. See you later, Miss Bristol."

"It's all right, Ben," she said, touching his hand and smiling. "Good luck with your mission, and I will see you on your return."

"Bye," was all Benedict could manage before she smiled again and vanished.

"Alright people!" yelled General Mickson suddenly. "Alright! It is exactly 08:00 hours and we have to drop now! System is guards drop first, followed by Macintyre, Nettlefold, Collington, and myself, and then it's the main armada. Assemble yourselves immediately in that order. We have to drop now!"

Benedict stood next to Commander Collington watching the attachment of guards stand in a horizontal line before the massive door. He shook numbly with fear at what was to happen.

The mechanic in charge of opening the door checked the men around the Drop Room to make sure that all wore their parachutes and he quickly glanced to make sure that everyone who wasn't supposed to be in there had left. Finally he walked quickly out the door and sealed it tightly behind him.

The intercom sounded: "General Mickson, this is Don here. We are positioned and ready for the drop."

"Thank you," replied the general, bracing himself. "Mechanic, proceed."

The door swung open and a gush of freezing air stormed in, showering the men. It was not as harsh as Benedict thought it would be – it was more like a breeze than a vortex trying to suck men out.

The guards jumped out, vanishing into the whiteness.

"Wait for it!" yelled General Mickson. "Wait for it! Wait for it! Now!"

Benedict ran and jumped, shutting his eyes and feeling the wind pass his face. He kept his eyes shut for a minute and then opened them again. He was staring at the clouds and the distant silhouettes of the security guards.

General Mickson was right next to him, the wind licking at his face. Dr Macintyre and Commander Collington were behind him.

They passed through the cloud layer and saw the Pacifica coast. It was beautiful with its trees and sand thickly condensed. The distant mountains beyond the trees offered food and water and fresh adventure.

General Mickson was pointing at something. Benedict strained to see what it was, but in the distance below him, he could see Port Dickens. Like the general's description it was located in a small rocky bay; the main settlement started on the beach-forest border and extended deep into the woods.

The guards below opened their parachutes. Benedict saw the silk shapes billow out. He wondered if he should open his own chute. He glanced at the general and, seeing him nod, pulled the cord.

A sudden pull was inflicted on him as the chute slowed him down, yanking his shoulders and chest harshly. Benedict gasped at this aggravation. General Mickson beside him displayed a look of pain as he opened his chute and, like he was pulled by a piece of elastic, hung at the same level as Benedict.

"We're getting close!" General Mickson yelled as the picturesque Port Dickens rose up to meet them. He spoke into his radio to the other guards and troops. "Guards, steer yourselves to the southern end of the beach and secure the immediate area. Remember, the second you touch down, unclip your gun. Main armada – "

Something had sailed past Benedict. He didn't know what it was, but gasped in horror when he saw the tiny bolt embedded in General Mickson's throat. Blood was gushing from the torn skin, pouring itself into his uniform as the general tried to remove the bolt, but without success. He choked, blood flecking in little droplets out of the puncture. Thick red blood was all over his face, all over his body, all over his ginger hair, his moustache, his abdomen. Blood – so much fucking blood: the first of much, much more.

"Oh, fuck!" Commander Collington cried as he pulled out his gun to ease the general's pain. But suddenly, a stream of bolts struck the general, severing his parachute. Mickson accelerated downwards, a true dead man.

"The enemy must know we're here!" screamed Dr Macintyre. He burst into his radio. "All troops we have bolts being fired at us from the ground. Get down as fast as you can to the beach. I repeat…"

But he stopped speaking when he saw the zeppelin. All could clearly see Omega Brotherhood soldiers on it. They weren't firing guns or bolts but just sitting there, hovering in the sky.

"What are they doing?" asked Collington.

Suddenly the zeppelin began to reverse at its maximum velocity. Benedict felt the rush of the reverse engines pushing against him. Then he realised what they were doing.

"Shit!" he grimaced. "They're using the engines to push us off course. They're gonna put us in the ocean. Then the guys on the beach will massacre the lot of us in one go."

"Emergency!" Macintyre yelled into the radio. "Divert course *against* the engines!" He strained on his chute cords to pull against the current. But it was useless, like trying to swim against a raging river.

The first of the guards struck the water, then the rest. Omega soldiers on the beach wasted no time in firing their guns. Grenades were shot out into the water.

The guards cried as they exploded, screaming as they turned into red dust.

"Jesus Christ!" cried Benedict as blood filled the blueness below.

Now it was their turn. Macintyre growled as he tried to steer the parachute away from the water but with no success. The three of them plunged in.

Benedict choked as water entered his mouth and travelled down his windpipe. He quickly discarded the parachute and swam up. He hit the surface. The first thing he saw was the Omega soldiers firing grenade after grenade, shedding more blood and blowing up more men.

He yelped when a severed arm fell onto his head. "Shit!" he shouted: blood was still pumping out of the limb, soaking his face. Crying with disgust, he threw it away.

"Sir!" cried a young voice beside him amidst the explosions.

It was a young red-haired guard.

"Sir, what do we do!" the guard screamed.

"We have to swim ashore and take the beach!" Benedict yelled as a grenade landed amongst a group of guards attempting to hide amongst a small cairn. He summoned another two guards, Macintyre and Collington. "Quickly! We have to seize the beach!"

"But the bombs will kill us all!" cried the young guard.

"That's a risk we'll have to take!" retorted Nettlefold. "Now, let's move!"

They began to swim towards the shore. It was easy, for the jumpsuits were equipped with buoyancy aids.

"Spread out!" roared Dr Macintyre. "Spread out!"

Suddenly a grenade landed near Benedict. He just managed to dive out the way, but as he twisted back he saw that the red-haired guard's face had been blown off, but he was still alive. Blood was flooding out of him as the faceless guard screamed and screamed and screamed like a baby.

"Shit!" barked Commander Nettlefold. "Keep going!" He could see the gunners on the shore now. They were thin men wearing the Omega uniform, but at the back and obviously commanding the gun crews, was a topless, heavily-built, muscular, bald sergeant yelling out orders to fire more grenades.

Benedict glanced upwards to see the main armada coming down. They had drawn their guns and fired at the gun crews. Commander Nettlefold used this opportunity to shout encouragement.

"Move on!" he yelled. "Move!"

The small platoon of guards continued to swim. The sandy floor was coming up to meet them and Benedict found he could wade. He unclipped his gun as he dashed ashore.

A corporal drew his knife and came to meet Benedict. But, quick as a flash, he drew his pistol and shot the corporal through the head, blood shooting out the other side of his skull onto the sand.

He fired a quick succession of shots at a grenade crew, killing them all. A soldier came running up to him carrying an axe and shrieking insults. Benedict just managed to stop his own execution by grabbing the handle of the axe with one hand and punching the soldier with the other. The soldier, not yet incapacitated, attempted to reach the Benedict's pistol lying on the sand.

"Take this," Nettlefold snarled as he smashed the axe into the side of the man's head. Blood erupted onto the sand as the top of the man's head was torn off. Benedict dropped the bloody axe and picked up his gun.

By now, Dr Macintyre and Commander Collington had arrived on the beach.

"We need to kill the rest of the gun crews," said Collington. "Let's go."

The troops dashed across the sand.

Benedict launched himself at a private and knocked him into the sand. The private attempted to shoot him, but the commander punched him and knocked him unconscious. He quickly grabbed back his pistol and shot down another gun crew.

With fewer guns and the crews distracted by the party on the sand, the waterborne soldiers could make their way to shore. A leading sergeant pushed past the bloody limbs and bodies lying in the water.

Suddenly from behind Benedict a guard was thrown hard against a wall, his spine snapping instantly. He soon saw the cause of this trouble: the burly, topless sergeant.

The first soldiers that arrived on the shore attempted to kill the sergeant. There was a scream as a young private was picked up by the burly sergeant. He screamed and begged for help from his comrades who were trying to seek help themselves…

"Oh – please!" the private suddenly pleaded. But the burly sergeant would have none of it. He lowered the private to the ground and smashed his face into a rock. The young private screamed as jaw was broken. But the burly sergeant smashed him into the rock face again and again, blood spurting everywhere. The private... was screaming! Then the burly sergeant picked him up for a final time and tossed his head back, snapping his neck.

Benedict snarled as the sergeant saw him. He aimed his pistol at the sergeant's head and fired. But nothing happened.

"Shit!" he cried, realising he had run out of bullets. He opened the barrel and loaded more in. He slapped the gun closed and aimed it again at the sergeant.

But instead, he found himself flying across the sand. The gun flew elsewhere.

"Alright you Epsilon piece of motherfucking shit!" the sergeant roared. "I'll teach ya how fighting's done!" He kicked Benedict in the chest. "And that's only a tap!"

Benedict stood up. Never defeated. He picked up a rifle and fired it, but the gun was also unloaded. "Fuck."

A group of Epsilon soldiers aimed their guns at the sergeant, but Benedict suddenly bellowed: "Lower your guns! This animal's mine!"

He landed a punch on the guard's jaw and kicked him in the abdomen.

The sergeant didn't even flinch. Instead he picked up Benedict by the collar and hurled him across the sand. He landed on his back and started to move away from the sergeant.

"You retreating, captain?" taunted the sergeant. He balled his fists and bent down to the commander.

"I ain't retreating!" said Benedict. Suddenly, he rolled over, snatched the sword from a dead lance corporal and plunged it into the sergeant's chest.

The burly sergeant collapsed onto his knees, his mouth open in a shocked gasp. Benedict stood and approached the sergeant.

"It's not 'captain'!" Benedict snarled to the sergeant. "It's *'commander'*! Commander Benedict Nettlefold."

Benedict thought about beheading the sergeant, but thought it better to walk off and let him die slowly. He glimpsed his gun and trod off towards it. He picked it up and then heard the sergeant get up. The burly man removed his own gun and pointed it at Benedict, but in a sudden swift movement, the commander turned around and fired three shots at the sergeant. The muscular man seemed to pause. For a second, Benedict thought that he wasn't dead and would come after him, but the sergeant fell forwards and hit the sand dead.

"That's what animals get," said Benedict.

The beach had been taken. Guards and soldiers regrouped for a brief rest. Benedict would have none of it. He summoned three guards to his attention.

"Get the rest of the soldiers together," he ordered. "We're going to plunder this port now."

While the three men dashed off, Nettlefold stared around, seeing for the first time that indeed this was a holiday resort. The Omega soldiers had stacked the deckchairs to the side, making way for their guns. There were several drinks and ice-cream stores that had been cleared for offices.

But this could never be a resort again after what had happened in the port. Benedict glanced with disgust into the sea. The port was red with blood and dotted with the limbs and bodies of the guards and a few of the soldiers.

"Fuck," he said with hatred towards the Omega soldiers. "You pieces of shit did this to those boys. Now I'm coming for you, you selfish animals."

"We're ready," said Commander Collington coming from down the beach, deeply dazed. "We'll follow you into battle, sir."

"Call me Benedict," said the dazed commander. He saw Collington smile at that. Then Nettlefold turned to the remaining armada and said in a confident manner: "Alright people, we've got a town to take."

Benedict led the way off the sand, charging into the seaside resort beyond. They'd entered the main promenade which was filled with Omega soldiers.

"Open fire!" Benedict roared as he ripped out his gun.

But the Omegans had prepared for this. They lobbed explosives at the charging troop. Fiery explosions filled the promenade and engulfed some of the unfortunate men and women.

"Fuck!" Benedict shouted as he threw himself down.

An Omega captain threw a pressure grenade at them; it landed in the thick of the party and exploded. Blood sprayed into the air and tapped the tarmac flood.

In less than a second, the beautiful sunlit promenade had transformed into a battlefield covered in thick blood. Several guards lay around on the floor motionless but alive. One of them was trying to reach for his gun, but without success, as, without him realising it, his fingers had been chewed off by the blast.

Benedict was being fired at, bullets sparking the ground beside him. Cursing loudly, he managed to roll himself into the garden of a pretty house. He took shelter behind the stone wall that separated it from the promenade.

He swore loudly as he surveyed the scene up ahead: the Omega soldiers had formed two lines, continually firing at the Epsilon soldiers, who had now thrown themselves behind boulders and walls like Benedict had. In the middle of the lines, there was a box of grenades being opened by a corporal.

Benedict had an idea. He needed to scatter the lines and create a distraction for the Epsilon soldiers to charge effectively. He aimed his pistol at the grenade box and pulled the trigger. For the next half second nothing happened. Benedict saw the corporal's face drop when he saw that a bullet had gone in. Then suddenly, the grenades erupted, creating a massive yellow fireball which shot sky-high, cooking the air.

The corporal and those next to him had been vaporised instantly, but those a fair distance screamed as the fireball burned them like paper scarecrows. The soldiers on the farthest ends were flung outwards into the trees and buildings; one of them was hurled high and then came crashing down on top of a roof.

"Forward!" yelled Benedict to everyone.

The dazed soldiers trudged along into the grey cloud created by the blast. Several screams sounded out as soldiers that had survived the blast, were shot.

As the smoke began to clear, Benedict glimpsed several more ice-cream shops and a hotel with a swimming pool at its front. The pool had been drained and some kind of mechanical console had been implanted inside. Benedict summoned Commander Collington and waved him over to the device.

"What do you reckon this is?" he asked Collington.

"I'm not sure; must be a control panel of some sort; maybe it controls the launcher that's been spotted in the town square. Quickly; we'd better stop that missile from being launched. Come on."

They continued to advance up the promenade, taking in as much as they could about the implanted devices. One entire house had been cleared and fitted with dozens of computers, and then fortified with rocket launchers and radar.

The square was directly up ahead. The largest open space in Port Dickens, it still seemed attractive: roses and grass filled the private gardens and hotel privets. The ground was still composed of the many bricks, wound into a pattern of a wave.

But in the centre of the square, over thirty Omega soldiers were overseeing the missile being checked by three technicians. What was surprising was that the missile was only two feet high – it was tiny. But why was it being guarded? And what was loaded inside?

A lance corporal saw the approaching soldiers first, coming out of the smoke like the living dead. He panicked and yelled at his comrades, but a single bullet caught him in the cheek. A captain gave the order to attack the Epsilon soldiers and they did so. But as they aimed their guns, Benedict fired every bullet, killing several of the nearby ones. Calmly, he reloaded his weapon and fired again, this time killing the captain.

Commander Collington and Dr Macintyre led the attack with Benedict in between them, who spied the technicians hiding throughout the launch pad.

He walked towards the pad, seeing the technicians crouching in the shear fear of what he could do to them.

One of them dropped before the commander's knees and begged for mercy. "Oh please, sir!" he whimpered. "Oh please – " Benedict kicked him in the chin and sent him flying across the pad. The other two made a run for it, but the commander sent two shots flying at them and they collapsed.

Suddenly a cheer rang out from the Epsilon soldiers.

The battle had been won.

Commander Collington and Dr Macintyre, both dirty and covered in blood from the fighting, cracked smiles. Benedict grinned back at them and looked down, noticing for the first time the amount of muck stained with dried blood that hung from his suit, especially the leg parts. He suddenly felt really hot, realising that he *was* in a thick leather suit and the sun was boiling. Up till now, the fighting had kept him preoccupied, but now that it was over, he could feel the sweat pouring from his body. His uniform would be soaked with it. But the worst thing was his jumpsuit was that perfectly dry.

Benedict turned on his radio. "Lieutenant Bilston, this is Commander Nettlefold. We've taken Port Dickens; all that needs doing now is disarming the missile. Apart from all that, mission is completed. Over."

There was no reply.

"Lieutenant Bilston, this is Commander Nettlefold. Please come in. Over."

Still no answer.

"Commander Collington," Benedict said, "is your radio working?"

"Yes. Is yours broken?"

"Yeah, I think so – "

"Commander!" one of the soldiers yelled, pointing to the mountains.

The *Levitator* was descending, great gusts of wind slapping together behind it. But something was wrong with it. At first, it seemed to be rocking slightly, but then the heavens screamed as the ship exploded into a fiery mess. The flames expanded outwards, tearing through the distant valleys. The wreckage seemed to do nothing at first, but then, like a burst balloon, it fell into the deep green trees.

Chapter 6   Crash Site Glory

Benedict cringed the moment he entered the flaming ruins of what was once the valiant *Levitator*, shouting continuously for survivors – but all that replied was the raw crackling of the flames. Commander Collington and Dr Macintyre jogged up behind him with the armada of men.

The *Levitator* had crashed near a tiny brook, practically vaporising any nearby trees and rendering the ground useless for wildlife. It didn't seem like a wood anymore; just a bleak rubbish site filled with fire.

Benedict frantically glanced around for some kind of body, but then he realised that he wasn't in the main body of the crash – this was just the outskirts: as one moved further up the slope, the heaps of rubble and fires grew taller, the pieces of shrapnel grew larger, until the massive burning skeleton of the *Levitator* stuck up from the ground, smoke pouring into the sky like the Black Death.

Benedict could only stare up at the tail in awe, wondering how anyone could have survived such a crash.

"Sir!" cried a soldier. "Here!" He was kneeling down beside a pile of shrapnel. Benedict could just see a body underneath.

"Help me get this off him," Benedict said, and the soldier helped him to lift the intertwined metal bars off the unfortunate soul beneath. They soon found out who it was: Chief Inspector Tame. The detective had a metal girder piercing into his neck. Burnt blood caked around the puncture. "Fuck," the commander whispered hoarsely, realising how much pain the detective must have gone through. Tame must've been like that for hours, unable to move, slowly choking to death, with the flames licking at his cheek.

Suddenly Benedict was filled with worry for Bristol. Rising up, he screamed, "Rachel!"

There was no reply amidst the roaring flames.

"Rachel!" he screamed again. "Rachel!"

"Will you please calm down?" muttered Dr Macintyre, coming up behind him. "If you keep on shouting and balling, the other trapped individuals will panic and attempt to escape the wreckage, resulting in accidental deaths. Now please - "

"Shut up!" barked Benedict suddenly, pushing Dr Macintyre hard in the chest, though with not enough force to make him fall, but merely to make him stumble. "Be quiet, alright? Don't annoy me, and shut your fucking mouth, you wanker!"

Benedict turned the other way and began to advance into the wreckage. Flames licked their way round his boots as the commander trudged through the remains. He glimpsed the piloting deck remnants, a smashed up container rammed against the ground. To his horror, the two pilots were plainly dead, crushed up. This made him panic even more.

"Rachel!" he bellowed into the fire. "Rachel!"

Suddenly, amidst the burning ruins, two figures staggered towards them. For a moment, Benedict thought that one of them might be Rachel Bristol, but, as the silhouettes became clearer, he saw them to be the Minuet and Professor Bentley.

The Minuet's royal costume had been badly singed and his boots scarred; Professor Bentley seemed more shocked than injured: his jaw was dropped in surprise, his hands curled like cannonballs, his hair a mess of dirt. Bentley's neat brown coat was badly charred and his tie only slightly singed.

"What happened?" gasped Dr Macintyre, approaching the Minuet. "Who fired at the *Levitator*?"

"We don't know," replied the Minuet in a hoarse whisper. "It came out of nowhere and hit us."

"What was it?" inquired Macintyre.

"Don't know," shrugged Professor Bentley.

"Where's Bristol?" Benedict asked nervously. "Where is she?"

Bentley sighed, slowly looking up at Benedict. "I last saw her running towards her quarters." He paused uneasily, for this would be hard to tell him. "Her quarters were the whereabouts of the weapon strike."

Benedict's heart sank.

She was dead.

The poor girl had perished.

"Fuckers," Benedict growled, now feeling true rage. "Omegans did this! Fucking Omegans!"

"Calm yourself, Commander," said the professor gently. "Calm down."

"I don't want to be calm!" screamed Benedict. "I want to get my hands on the bunch of those Omega soldiers that launched the weapon and kill 'em myself!" The image of the servant Bradley suddenly popped into his mind; he'd said that Dr Macintyre was Omegan – that was good enough for Benedict…

"They'll have gone by now," said the Minuet quietly. "No point in going after them."

"That's all right," said Benedict, the pattern of his voice betraying the fact that his temper was rising. "D'you know why? Cos we've got one of the fuckers right here…" The commander removed his gun and aimed it at Dr Macintyre's chest.

"I hope this isn't another one of those things with you again," replied Macintyre, gazing down at the gun. "Because if it is, then you're dead."

"It's not 'one of those things'," Benedict replied with no emotion. "A few weeks ago, a servant approached me, said he knew quite a bit about you – he mentioned that you were an 'ex-Omegan'. He did!"

"What the devil are you on about?" Dr Macintyre stuttered. "Taking the word of a mere servant against me?"

"His word seemed better than yours."

"You could be shot for this!" stammered Macintyre.

"Funny, because I've got the gun here," sneered Benedict. In one swift movement he cocked the weapon. He raised the gun to Macintyre's forehead and pressed it against the bridge of his nose.

"Please," stammered Dr Macintyre, "put the gun down."

Everyone stared in sheer fear at the sight of the commander, Benedict Nettlefold, pointing his famous pistol at Dr Macintyre. Sweat and dirt was matted on Benedict's face, his dark brown eyes reflecting the surrounding flames. He was that dark figure in this dark world.

"Why should I? After what you've done to me, why should I bow down to you?" A tear crept to the corner of Nettlefold's eye. "Why do you hate me so much? When first we met, you appeared to have nothing against me, but all that time, you despised me. And that led to you trashing my wedding and taking my Adeline into your arms. Now you see me making friends with Rachel and you want to ruin that. First you try to assassinate me in my quarters, but that failed, so you have a missile launched at the ship, and you kill her and nearly everyone else. I wondered why you parachuted down to the battle – it was a logical assumption that you were required due to your qualifications as a field medic. I sensed you were nervous before we dropped; at first, I dismissed it, mistaking it for the fear of battle, but I now realise why you were nervous: you wanted to destroy the entire ship, kill everyone onboard – takes some courage, you know. But you did it – just so you could express your hatred towards me. You're a fucking tosser."

"Come on, Commander, that's absolutely ridiculous," said Dr Macintyre. "Listen, old son, you're mistaken. That's going too far. Even if I hated you that much, I just wouldn't go that far, mate. I just wouldn't."

"Benedict," said Commander Collington, approaching him. "Put the gun down. Put it down. Ben, we've survivors to find. Put the weapon down."

"No."

"Is this what Rachel would want?" said the Minuet. "Ask yourself that."

"It's not a matter of what she wants anymore," Benedict whispered. "It's a matter of what *I* want."

Professor Bentley was next to step in. "Commander, I'm afraid I might have exaggerated before – I'm not sure *exactly* where the weapon hit. She might still be alive, a very small chance, but there is a chance."

"The sooner we start searching," said Macintyre, "the greater our chances of finding her alive – so I really would appreciate you putting the gun down now!"

"Yeah," Collington chimed in. "Commander, we want to find her ASAP, don't we?" But the commander kept the pistol raised. "Put the gun down," he cried, now panicking. "For God's sakes man, put the gun down!"

"If you ever hurt an Epsilon," snarled Benedict at the dazed Macintyre, "or if I find evidence that you are an Omegan, I'll kill you." He disarmed the gun and returned it to his holster.

Suddenly one of the guards yelled at them.

"What is it?" said Benedict, alarmed. He dashed down to where the guard was: by a pile of rubble.

"We found someone," said the guard, lifting off the metal chunks.

Benedict glanced down and his heart filled with joy, because underneath the rubble, bleeding but alive in her torn uniform, was Bristol.

"Rachel!" Benedict cried gleefully. At once, he began tearing off the metal, not stopping until Rachel was completely free. He dragged her out, and then lifted her up into his arms.

"Benedict," she whispered with dry lips, "is that you?"

"Yes it is," replied Commander Nettlefold. A guard handed him a bottle of water which he gently poured onto her lips. "Better?" he asked when she'd drunk a bit.

"Much better," she answered. "I might be able to stand."

Benedict lowered her slowly, allowing her feet to touch the ground in a soft kiss. She stood without any difficulty to Benedict's relief – she hadn't broken a leg. But then she saw the dead body of Chief Inspector Tame and screamed. She ran away from the commander and towards Tame's body.

"No! No! No!" she cried, falling down beside the corpse. "Please God, no! Not him!"

"I'm sorry," said Benedict, dropping to his knees beside her and stroking her hair lightly. "I'm so sorry, but he's dead. I couldn't save him."

"What d'you mean you couldn't?" she snapped suddenly. "He was alive not that long ago! You could've got to him! You could have saved him!" Tears streamed down her face. "I hate you, Benedict! I hate you! I hate you!"

"Please, Rachel."

"How dare you call me by my first name, Nettlefold! Go away, I mean it, piss off!" She shoved him hard. "Leave me alone! Get fucked somewhere else! Go! Go!"

"Alright, detective," said Benedict, quite humiliated, backing away slowly. "Alright." He stood up and trudged back towards the wreckage. The other guards and soldiers pretended not have heard what happened, but two of them couldn't help sniggering in the corner. Benedict scowled at them, causing them to go about their business.

"Benedict," cried a hoarse whisper from nearby. Nettlefold turned around frantically to see who it was. But no one was there.

"I'm here," cried the voice again.

Benedict turned to see Lieutenant Bilston lying against a bulkhead. Sweat was sandwiched to his face, and anyone could tell he had been hit by something. Blood was leaking down his lips.

Benedict dashed over to him and crouched down. "You okay?" he asked.

"I've been hit," he said, blood gurgling out his mouth as he unclasped his hands to reveal a spike sticking through him. He looked at Benedict, tears gouging down his once strong face. "Son," he whispered weakly, "you have to complete this mission."

"We will," said Benedict, gripping both his arms. "Commander Collington!" he shouted. "Get over here!"

"Please, commander," Lieutenant Bilston cried, "listen to me. You have to stop Lord Marius: he's got a weapon that could kill millions. You have to prevent him from using it."

"What weapon?"

"Jesus Christ!" gasped Commander Collington as he approached them with Dr Macintyre. Bentley and the Minuet were not far behind. Macintyre examined the wound in Lieutenant Bilston's chest. He touched the spike, but, seeing the lieutenant flinch, retracted his hand. Blood dribbled onto Bilston's uniform from his mouth. He coughed, causing more red to squeal down his chin.

"Easy, Lieutenant," said Dr Macintyre, using his tissue to wipe the sticky stuff off Lieutenant Bilston's face.

Suddenly, Lieutenant Bilston grabbed Benedict by the collar, more blood erupting from his mouth. "Listen," he said through bloody gritted teeth. "Listen to me – you must stop Lord Marius. He's got something, Benedict, something that has grave consequences for mankind. Stop him, Commander Nettlefold. Stop him." More blood poured out his mouth, only now it wasn't thin and runny, but thick and viscous.

"What has he got?" asked Benedict.

"Commander, please, I need to ask him some medical questions," said Dr Macintyre sternly, and seeing Benedict's angered eyes, stuttered quickly: "Surely you can see the sense in me assessing his condition." He turned his attention back to Bilston. "You will make it, Lieutenant. You can and you shall make it, sir. I shall try and send a distress signal and get help here ASAP. You will make it, sir, you will make it."

"No I won't," said Lieutenant Bilston. "Just make sure you complete the mission. Complete it." Suddenly, he choked and more blood drooled down his chin. Slowly his eyes shut and soon Bilston was dead.

As the day passed, more bodies were recovered, most of them dead. The majority of them were the servants and maids, however, there were a few guards and crewmembers amongst the deceased. Several of them had been unfortunate enough to be standing by a pod of containers holding highly pressurised gas; they were found missing limbs – one of them had had the top of his head sliced open, the piece of metal sliced into his skull like a sabre.

But there were surviving guards and servants. Dr Macintyre had them sent straight into Port Dickens where everyone would stay for the night.

Benedict had assumed command of the party – much to Macintyre's and the Minuet's disapprovals. Dr Macintyre thought he was 'unfit and lousy' to lead such a team, and the Minuet stated that he outranked him. However, Commander Collington came to Benedict's defence, saying that he, the Minuet, was a royal figure, not part of the military, and although Benedict had the same rank as himself, Commander Nettlefold had more experience than he did. So, as a result, Benedict took command.

Benedict headed into Port Dickens later that evening. It was a clear sky and the first stars were beginning to show, bright twinkling spots of infinite beauty. But they very far away from the human race – they had problems of their own; Benedict decided to focus on his own problems: he needed to get the jumpsuit off: it was clinging onto him.

He began to undo the tight straps and remove it, but with greater difficulty than putting it on: the sweat produced by his body had formed a glue between him and the suit.

"Fuck," he cursed grumpily. "Fucking worthless shit – made by fucking idiots." He removed the thick jumpsuit boots and began to peel off the rest of the suit. He grimaced with disgust at the sight of the sheer sweat soaked through his uniform. He had trouble trying to get the suit off from round his shoes, as the sweat had caused it to tighten severely around the ankles. Nevertheless, he managed so, and threw the suit over his arm when he'd taken it off. He grudgingly discovered that he now had nowhere to put his pistol, so, cursing deeply, he removed the holster from the jumpsuit. There was a menial belt attached to it, so he ripped it off with the holster and fastened them both round his waist.

It wasn't a bad holster and belt really. The belt *was* a little bit plain but efficient; however, the holster was beautifully made. Back in the Drop Room onboard the *Levitator*, he hadn't the time to admire its beauty, but now, as he slid his pistol into it, he noticed in detail the carvings on the leather. The strap which held the gun in place clipped onto the holster in such a way that you could run your hand along it and it would gently undo itself.

Yes, the holster was incredible: perfect for use in battle.

Satisfied, Benedict headed into Port Dickens, a steady glow emitting from the main square to which the commander headed directly for.

The missile had been removed, and in its place a campfire had been set up; orange faces reflected its heat and light. They were all staring up at Benedict, Macintyre included, waiting for orders, although the good doctor only listened in unwillingly.

Benedict stared back, positioning himself on a small crate, so everyone could see him. He put the jumpsuit and boots to one side, and then turned his attention back to the crowd. He wasn't sure how he was going to say this to the remaining team, but he knew that he had to mention it in one form or another.

"As the newly appointed leader," he said, "it's dawned on me how uncertain you all are of the present situation. I know you all have a lot of questions and I have the answer. When Lieutenant Bilston died, he told me that this Lord Marius has some sort of weapon. He said that we have to stop him using it. Now, I wouldn't normally take heed of this from your average fucked-up lieutenant, but in light of what's just happened, we should embark on this new quest – sorry, mission: times of adventure are over."

"So where the fuck are we going?" asked a soldier from the back of the gathering.

"Mind your language!" Dr Macintyre said quite loudly.

"Don't tell me not to swear!" retorted the soldier.

"Shut up!"

"No, I bloody won't – medic's bloody galore! Always get their way…"

"How dare you… Apologise!"

"Very well," said the soldier – better not challenge the medic.

"We're going further inland," replied Benedict, trying to move on from the argument. "We need to stop this Marius, because if we don't, he might try and unleash this weapon."

"What weapon is this?" asked someone.

Benedict, gazing down, grimaced slightly. He stared up again and said without emotion: "Something that could fuck up a lot of people. We have to stop it. Now, as Dr Macintyre has already mentioned, we stay here tonight – get plenty of rest; you'll need it. Tomorrow we take the pass through the mountains and head further inland."

"Benedict," said Commander Collington, "may I make a further recommendation?"

"Go ahead."

"Before we embarked on this mission, I took liberty of studying the map of Pacifica, including the area around Port Dickens." He pointed towards the distant mountains. "Up there," he explained, "are the Streak Mountains; they make a complete route around the island, as I'm sure most of you know. In those mountains is a valley named Streak Valley which is a clear path out of the range. If we took it, it would cut several days off our journey, and save us having to climb up and down mountain tops."

Benedict seemed impressed, but Professor Bentley was shaking his head. "There's a problem with Mr Collington's recommendation, sir," he said. "Streak Valley isn't a children's playground – the Lambda Brotherhood once used it as a biological weapons storage facility. Then one day the weapons were triggered, and everyone there died within days. It would be most foolish to enter that biohazard area, even after a long time since the weapons went off; if we do so, we run the risk of becoming infected with something nasty. That's what finished the Lambdas off, because three of their top generals were there and got infected. As a matter of fact – "

"Okay professor," snarled Collington, "we know our history."

"You think I'm treating you all like the uneducated?" retorted Bentley.

"Will you two just shut your fucking traps?" barked Benedict. "Professor Bentley's right: there might be bio remnants; however, it would be even more dangerous to attempt climbing the mountains –"

"But – "

" – *especially* since we are a large group and we have no proper climbing equipment, Dr Bentley. It would therefore be impossible to ensure everyone's safety." Benedict paused calmly, although quite uneasily. "Tomorrow, we shall pass through this 'Streak Valley'."

Dr Macintyre didn't like a word of this. He suddenly leapt up and challenged Benedict: "Commander, have you lost your mind?!"

"Calm down, my dear man," said Benedict sarcastically, pleased that Dr Macintyre was losing control – for once, it was the good doctor's turn. That animal had made Benedict lose his control, his prospects and himself; now, Macintyre was the one who had lost his calm. Now he would make a show of himself.

"You can't just stroll into Streak Valley like you own the place!" cried Dr Macintyre.

"Silence, doctor," sneered Benedict.

"Don't *you* tell me to be silent!" shouted Macintyre. "Don't *you* tell me to shut my fucking mouth!" Poor Dr

Macintyre seemed rather uncomfortable: he hadn't removed his jumpsuit yet and sweat was soaking his face, neck, his whole body. Macintyre's blond hair was a mess of dirt and thick black mud that clung to his sweat-stricken forehead.

"Not well, doctor?" Benedict said, although with a hint of cruelty in his voice. "I suggest that you either lie down or just belt the fuck up, you selfish brat!" Now the commander had returned to his old self, bad-tempered and full of hatred.

"Don't you dare speak to me like that!" Dr Macintyre replied loudly. "Just because I'm engaged to your ex-girlfriend …"

"How dare you," growled Benedict, slowly advancing towards the doctor.

Commander Collington quickly placed himself between the two. "Benedict," he said quietly, "calm down son."

"Get out of my way, Commander!" snapped Benedict. "Get out of my *fucking* way!"

"Come on," replied Collington, "think about what you're doing. Please, Commander, you've already threatened him once today already."

Benedict shot his eyes sadistically at the medic: the man who'd ruined him, the man who'd stripped him of stripes, a wife, and his pride.

Now this man stood before him a miserable wreck of sweat, fever and tears.

Chapter 7   Marius & Co.

Lord Marius was never one to be questioned, nor one to question other people – unless of course they withheld extremely vital information relating to his own plans.

As he sat atop of the long table, gazing blankly at its dark wooden surface, he remembered one of his forgotten errands that day: sending a patrol to a nearby village to put down a tiny vendetta between the locals. It was nothing to him, but he didn't want to risk any sort of rebellion – never mind, that could be tomorrow's task.

A flash of lightening from outside signalled the beginning of another storm, one of many. A sensible man would've gotten inside the fortress, but not Lord Marius: no, he liked this small hut that he and his associate were taking dinner in. Normally they had their evening meal in a large banquet hall in the centre of the castle, but tonight they were having it inside the hut.

It wasn't a bad hut really: a small rectangular building made of rotting wood and a tin-can roof that echoed the sound of raindrops. It was situated on the hill behind the castle. It comprised of three rooms: a small entrance porch with cobwebs on the ceiling light, the main room in which Lord Marius and his associate were seated, and adjoining to the main room was a tiny galley in which a single cook mashed their stew.

He raised his eyes upwards, seeing that his associate, Professor Davenport, was bored and irritated: his elbows were rested on the table and his fingers were crossed in a steeple; every so often he would flinch as if the hut wall was prodding him on his back.

"Why do you keep doing that?" remarked Lord Marius.
"What, sir?"
"That!" Lord Marius snapped. "You keep fidgeting! Why?"

Professor Davenport knew it was no use trying to conceal his distaste for this filthy hut in front of Lord Marius. "This hut!" he cried finally. "It's just so... incredibly... *dirty*!"

"I apologise if you do not like it," said Lord Marius, "alas I thought we'd have a delicious local dish tonight. The steward told me that it's best served in 'a room away from luxury' – apparently anyway... Whether he was speaking bollocks, I don't know. But anyway, professor, I thought this hut'd do."

"I still think you made a wrong decision, sir. How many times do you wish to do this?"

"A few," replied Lord Marius. "Don't worry, it's not that dirty!"

"But sir, these book cases are made of rot itself – just look!" Professor Davenport stood up and examined a bookshelf. "Look at this, sir!" He took out a brown book and, opening it, remarked: "Looks like another forgotten text, sir. Hmm, it is entitled: *Build A Life* by, author's name is rubbed out, sir."

Lord Marius laughed loudly. "Come, sit down, professor! I think that our cook has finished this delicious stew!"

The cook appeared out of the galley carrying two rough bowls of the dark stew. He set them down at their places, and then dashed back into the kitchen. He emerged for a second time with a bottle of wine and two goblets. He filled them and then whispered something in Lord Marius's ear.

"Thank you for the advice, my friend," replied Lord Marius, "but I still think we'll have our dinner here. Continue with our dessert preparations."

"Yes sir," said the cook re-entering the galley.

"What is it?" inquired Professor Davenport.

"Apparently," said Lord Marius, "there is a flood of muddy rainwater coming down the mountain. Our friend back there says he's seen it from the galley window, but I'm still intent on finishing my dinner."

"But sir - "

"We are in no danger!" Lord Marius shouted, though with little anger. "Just eat your food, professor."

Professor Davenport knew better than to argue with Lord Marius. Silently, he began to consume his stew and drink his wine. Outside the never-ending rain continued to lash against the windows and the lightening continued to spark the blackened sky.

Lord Marius was someone to enjoy his food – wherever he was; even if it was howling with rain outside, he always made sure that he enjoyed his food. Professor Davenport didn't like the idea of disrupting his meal, but when there was a threatening flood outside, he tended to break this respect. But he decided it wasn't worth it – besides, the stew was delicious.

"What's on the agenda for tomorrow?" Davenport enquired.

"I've got to send that bloody patrol to that village," Lord Marius sighed.

"Locals kicking up havoc again?"

"Yeah, they're heavily intent on having their damned vendetta," said Lord Marius quietly. "I'm not particularly interested in their affairs, but when it concerns the safety of my tight fist, I must intervene."

"How do you mean?"

"Well, a small vendetta can easily escalate into something much worse – we don't want a siege." Marius leant back on his chair, the stew quite finished. He scratched his black beard and ran his hand through his dark hair – he was quite stressed after a long days work.

And it had been a long day indeed. There had been so much paperwork: bills, letters of interest – and of course, complaint letters from angry Pacifican residents, very angry ones indeed.

And that was why Lord Marius had wanted to eat his evening meal in this hut, something away from the castle. It was a dirty little place, but it was a small break from politics.

Finally, when they had both finished their meals, the cook took away their dishes and goblets. He came back a few minutes later with a small box, like the type with wedding rings in; but there seemed to be no gold in this one.

"What is that?" Professor Davenport asked, deeply puzzled at this little box.

"This," said Lord Marius, "is our dessert."

"What do you mean, sir?"

"You'll see," he said. "Cook, you may leave us."

"Yes, my lord," whispered the cook, picking up his coat and vanishing into the rain.

Lord Marius waited until he had walked a good distance away from the hut and then opened the tiny box. Inside was a tiny red jewel, no bigger than a tooth. It gleamed in spite of the dull light in the hut. Beside the jewel was a small scrap of yellow paper. Lord Marius picked it out, unfolded it and read out loud:

"To the dear fellow who purchases this:

"Charm up your party or ball with a few lovely ladies! They're beautiful, gorgeous, and charming. Simply press the ruby."

"Where did you get that from, sir?" Professor Davenport stammered.

"The local market," replied Lord Marius happily. "I thought it would make dessert…"

"Are you sure about this, sir?"

Lord Marius smiled and shut the box. "No, Dr Davenport, it's too early yet. I think midnight would suit me best…"

Suddenly someone burst into the room, their rough feet scraping on the dusty floor. It was Major Regan, commanding officer of Lord Marius's Omegan army. Sweat streamed down his orange face and his uniform was soaked with the rain. He stood straight to attention before the two men.

"Don't you know manners, Mr Regan?" said Lord Marius in a fairly strict manner.

"Sorry, my lord," said Major Regan, "for bursting in on you in this hour, but I have important news, concerning Port Dickens."

"What about it?" said Lord Marius, still angered by Major Regan's sudden appearance.

"The Epsilon Brotherhood has seized control."

"Damn!" shouted Lord Marius. "Fucking bastards! You said that Port Dickens was well fortified, Mr Regan!"

"I did, my lord," said the major calmly, "and indeed it was. The zeppelin in the sky managed to push the invasion party into the bay where grenade launchers fired on them. But somehow they made it to the beach."

"Somehow?" roared Lord Marius. "What in hell's name do you mean, *somehow*?"

"My lord, we did destroy their ship, so they can't – "

"I'm not interested in their fucking ship! Just tell me how the fuck they made it to the shore!"

"Well, my lord, one man escaped, a private, and was picked up by the zeppelin later. He reported that the party was led by a commander by the name of Benedict Nettlefold."

"Shit," snarled Lord Marius. "How the fuck did that man ever lead an armada?"

"My guess sir is that the leading general was killed in the descent and this commander was next in the chain of command."

"Where is this private?" asked Lord Marius.

"He is in the porch," said Major Regan.

"Send him in."

"Yes, my lord," Major Regan responded, turning to the door. "Private!" he shouted. "Enter at the double!"

A skinny individual marched stiffly into the room and saluted Lord Marius.

"Name," whispered the lord.

"Hawkins, sir; Private Hawkins, sir."

"You say that this Benedict Nettlefold led the onslaught," stated Lord Marius. "How did you know who he was?"

"Recognised him, my lord," informed Private Hawkins. "We met before, a few years ago."

"How?"

"During a banquet, my lord. We talked, but only briefly. My lord, I must inform you of another individual whom I recognised."

"You have a recognition gift," smiled Lord Marius, though the grin was slightly dull.

"I only recognised two people, my lord, and the second person is someone quite famous."

"Who was it?"

Private Hawkins shuddered a little. "I gravely inform you, my lord that Dr Macintyre is on these shores."

"Oh fuck," said Lord Marius. Now it was his turn to shiver. His most lethal enemy had come for him – probably to finish the job started all those years ago. "Private Hawkins, why did you let him get away? Now he will come for this castle and finish us!"

"My lord, we were outnumbered. I beg of you, my lord, to hear that I tried to stop him but could not."

"Your pistol," said Lord Marius, "how long is its range?"

"Five hundred yards, my lord."

"When you saw the doctor, was he within five hundred yards?"

"Yes, my lord."

"Did you have your gun on you at that particular time."

"Of course, my lord."

"Was it loaded?"

"My lord, it was."

"Then you could've taken a shot at him, yet you didn't."

"My lord – "

"That is unacceptable, private!" yelled Lord Marius. Suddenly, he snatched Major Regan's sword from his belt and thrust it through the private's cheek.

Blood vomited onto the floor as the shocked Private Hawkins collapsed. Lord Marius ripped the sword out and handed it back to Major Regan.

"Inform your men," said Lord Marius, "that the next one who fails me will receive the exact same treatment. Get the undertakers to take away the body. Now, I want you to stop this Dr Macintyre. They will have to pass through the mountains in order to reach here – find them and fucking stop them! Understood? Dismissed!"

"Yes, my lord!" said Major Regan. He saluted, and then disappeared swiftly.

"Why did you do that?" said Professor Davenport, shocked deeply.

"I can't take any chances; the men need to be kept in harsh discipline. Now, to more important matters – with the light of Dr Macintyre's arrival, Project Vindication needs to be placed at top priority – I want another test within the next few days."

"I understand, sir, but the antimatter cylinders aren't quite ready for another test."

"Then make them ready!" said Lord Marius. "I want another test soon, so we can stop this Dr Macintyre and his bunch of lubberly bandits."

"My lord, you have reminded me of another point of which I wish to make."

"Go ahead."

"Sir, I strongly recommend against weaponizing black light."

"Professor, you've mentioned this a hundred times."

"My lord," whispered Davenport, "I know you're sick and tired of me saying this, but you remember a few months ago when we did the first experiment, when we obtained a minuscule amount of black light, initially smaller in volume than a proton – you saw how it expanded, filling the entire chamber. We barely managed to stop it. If we start weaponizing the stuff…"

"My dear, professor, I am aware of the risks associated with it."

"My lord, it is fine to be aware of the risks associated with experiments, but to weaponize the deadliest stuff we've ever seen would be foolish."

"Professor Davenport, I know the risks. Dismissed."

"Yes, my lord."

Lord Marius watched the professor leave, and then gazed down at the box. Should he press the jewel? He decided not, for another day's work had taken its toll.

Chapter 8   Streak Valley

It was the heat of the day as the companions made their way down into Streak Valley. Sweat poured down all of their faces, through their clothes, into their boots, making them all feel extremely uncomfortable – apart from Dr Macintyre that is: he had managed to sneak into the ruins of the *Levitator* and retrieve some of his equipment, including some kind of cream that prevented sweat from remaining around for too long. He was trudging along near the front, quite happily.

Benedict was leading the group. He carefully lowered himself down jagged rocks, letting others behind know of any danger. He was glad to be out of that terrible jumpsuit, but had still retained the boots, as they provided good hiking material.

Chief Inspector Bristol was right behind him with Professor Bentley, Commander Collington, Macintyre, and the irascible Minuet. They were all tired and sore, but they knew it would be over soon. They could see Streak Valley below them, not a huge distance down, but they still had to traverse these horrid, jagged cliffs.

Benedict wiped the sweat from his forehead, seeing the steep cliff face ahead.

"Shit," he muttered quietly. "How the fuck are we going to navigate this?" The cliff face was incredibly smooth, hardly any grooves in it at all. He lowered his head, but there were no escaping the sight: the cliff ran down into the black nothingness of a pothole. Benedict strained his eyes, but he couldn't see the bottom.

He turned his head and shouted: "Halt! Everyone halt!"

It took time for message to travel down the long line, but eventually the whole party stood still, waiting for Benedict. The commander perched himself on a large piece of quartz, so the expedition could see him.

"Alright," he said loudly, "we have a slight problem. Ahead of us is an extreme cliff face that drops… I don't know what the fuck it drops in to – but the fact of the matter is that we have to cross over the drop. The path continues on the other side, so once over we should be able to make it safely to Streak Valley."

"Question," said Dr Macintyre. "What are we supposed to grip onto?"

"Here," said Professor Bentley, handing over a coil of rope.

Benedict examined it: coarse and very thin. It could snap. However, there was little choice in the matter. He tied the rope around his waist, being certain that it was secure.

"What d'you think you're doing?" said Bristol suddenly.

"Ah, so now you ask…" Benedict made sure he was sarcastic with this reply. He smiled at her, but not with your usual friendly smile. He handed the end of the rope to Professor Bentley. "Right, prof," he said, "attach your end of the rope to…" He spied a sharp spike of rock beside him. "… this pillar here."

He glanced ahead at the cliff, and then turned around to the rest of the party. "Okay, I'm going to climb across the cliff face and tie the rope on the other side. Once I've done this, you can begin coming over one by one. Grab onto the rope as tight as you can and put your feet in the grooves. Here goes…"

Benedict's heart leapt like an earthquake as he extended a foot over the dark void. He searched frantically for a foothold, eventually finding a small cranny embedded on the rock. His foot slid into it easily, but small grains of dust flew down into the darkness below. Now he needed to swing his other foot round and slam it into that second groove a few feet away.

This was what he hesitant about.

He stared down into the darkness. Suddenly a voice inside his head screamed:

"Go for it!"

Hesitantly, Benedict reached out with his second foot and swung his body around. He shut his eyes tightly, bracing for the fall – but instead he found himself quite happily clinging to the face.

"Shit," he grinned back at the expedition. "Fucking shit, I ain't fuckin' dead. I guess that complete wanker up there doesn't want to deal with me just yet…"

Then the troublesome thought of how he would have to get his first foot into the foothold where his second foot was and then get his second foot out and into the third groove at the same time came to him. What a fuckload…

And he did just that.

"Phew!" he cried. Risking a glance behind him, he realised that the end wasn't that far. "How the fuck am I gonna do this?" he sniffed. He gulped and then suddenly flung himself backwards, landing spread-eagled on the rock.

"You okay?" Professor Bentley asked from the other side.

"Fucking brilliant!" shouted Benedict, launching himself up, a gleeful smile on his face. "Fucking Paris whores, I did it!" Benedict untied the rope from around him, and then retied it round the small pillar of rock. He tugged it briefly to make sure it was tight.

"Alright!" he called across to the other side. "Listen carefully: keep your legs tightly wrapped around the rope and slowly let yourself fall so that your back is facing downwards; then, slow as fuckin' possible, inch yourself along the rope. It should be tight enough for you all to make it safely. Okay?"

Professor Bentley went across first – his timid figure a dot against the blackness beneath. "Fuck," he snarled about halfway across.

Benedict laughed: "That's the first time I've heard you swear, professor!"

"Shut your fucking mouth!" Professor Bentley retorted. "Or I'll fuse it together with one of my grand plasma inventions, so you'll never be able to tell a woman you love her – you'll have to do it with your shagging parts!"

"Alright!" sniggered Benedict. He reached out his hand and helped the professor onto the other side.

"I didn't mean it really," said Professor Bentley, beaming.

"Yeah right…"

Dr Macintyre was the next to go across.

It was sudden.

Like a volcano erupting.

Benedict lost his temper.

"How are you doing, Dr Macintyre?" sneered the commander. "Don't fall whatever you do – there won't be any more victims for you down there."

"What are you talking about?" cried Macintyre, deeply puzzled.

"I'm talking about how you're such a fucking stupid tosser!" shouted Benedict. "Fuck you!"

"Calm down, Benedict!" cried the doctor. "Please calm down, okay?"

"Just wait 'til you get to the other side… I'll soddin' kill you."

Dr Macintyre began to hurry across now. Sweat *was* pouring from his body now. His clammy fingers struggled to grip the rope. His brown boots hung in the air, the dirty soles showing themselves to the sky. Eventually the good doctor made his way across the pothole, and used his eternal strength to straighten himself up and look Benedict in the eye.

"Don't *ever* do that again," Macintyre snarled. "Have I made myself absolutely clear?"

"Certainly, Mr Macintyre."

"*Dr* Macintyre!" the medic screamed. "Now straighten your backside up and help the others get across!"

"Yes, sir." Benedict watched the enraged medic go to the edge of the dark pit and help Bristol off the rope. He saw him whisper something in her ear; the detective glanced up at the commander with a look of distaste in her eyes.

Dr Macintyre had succeeded in turning someone else against him.

For the next hour, the entire party was helped across the pit. No one fell into the void, thankfully. Professor Bentley was that particular individual who was petrified of big long drops: particularly those ones that didn't really end.

When the entire team was across, Benedict pushed ahead to the front. He was quite pushy when he passed by Dr Macintyre, angrily flinging him out of the way.

"Okay folks," said the commander, "we're ready to press on. Pick up your guns and let's get our asses into Streak Valley ASAP."

Streak Valley was the same as it always was.

A deserted land of white sand that stretched as far as the eye could see. There was nothing in it – not one speck of life, apart from a tiny pile rubble in the distance.

The second the party set foot into the valley, Benedict tried to see what it was, but no: it remained a tiny pile of rubble.

He turned to Professor Bentley next to him and inquired as to what it was.

"It's probably just the remains of that Lambda base; you know, the one that was completely destroyed…"

The commander looked upwards as the last of the expedition descended off the rock. There were sighs of relief as they found that they no longer had to climb jagged peaks – or navigate over potholes. Now, it was quite literally a walk in the park.

Nevertheless, there was something about Streak Valley that made Benedict worry. It was more of a feeling than anything. Nevertheless, he double-checked that his gun was loaded.

The Minuet grasped his sword tightly, as if sensing the same thing.

Benedict saw this, and then said to the expedition: "Let's get across this fucking valley."

He began to lead the way into the white void. Behind him the expedition followed suit in single file as though they were walking along a narrow beam with a deep pit on either side.

An hour passed. Then two.

The pile of rubble had turned out to be remnants of a bulkhead, most probably when the *Levitator* exploded, judging that the metal was not rusty and the impact marks in the ground looked fresh.

But there was still no sign of the other end. And the expedition *was* becoming tired. Dr Macintyre slapped more of that cream of his on. The Minuet seemed irritated: he scratched his bald head frustratingly. Commander Collington was in deep conversation with Professor Bentley about the incident of the valley. As for Bristol: she was just so pissed off with the whole thing that she trudged along in silence, completely oblivious to her surroundings.

"Minuet," said Benedict suddenly, "how far d'you reckon?"

"Don't know," said the royal figure. "Streak Valley is massive. I don't know whether we'll get there today or tomorrow, or the next day."

"I'll call a rest in a moment," said Benedict. "I want some ground covered first though."

"Sure, Commander Nettlefold."

And that was when he felt it. A slight tremor in the ground.

"What was that?" Benedict wondered. He stared back at the long line of the expedition. Everyone had felt it. But nothing else happened.

"Ignore it," said Dr Macintyre to the troupe. "It's probably just a minor earthquake or something like that."

Everyone began walking again.

"He's right," said Professor Bentley who was now walking right behind Benedict. "Quake's occur frequently in this mountain range."

"Well that's good news," said Benedict – he knew why Bentley had come up to talk to him: the professor didn't want to be caught in the middle of *another* fight between him and Macintyre –

"Or it might've been some kind of rockslide," continued Bentley. "Did you know that there are these types of rock flows that behave just like rivers, and no one really knows why? Aye, it's incredible. The other thing that could've caused it is the blast created by booster engines on a zeppelin – "

Suddenly Benedict wheeled around. "What did you say?"

"Oh, the rock flows! Yes, they have this – "

"No! No! The bit after that."

"Zeppelins?"

"Yes – tell me about that."

"Well," said Bentley, "when a zeppelin needs to get away in a hurry, it can activate its booster engines – "

"Everyone, take cover!" screamed Benedict. "Take cover now!"

Suddenly explosions ringed around them, fiery balls reaching into the clouds. Benedict threw himself on top of the professor and pushed them both to the ground.

He heard cries as enemy soldiers hit the ground. "Get the hell out of here!" he whispered to the professor.

Benedict stood up and found himself staring straight into the face of an Omega warrior. A golden sword glittered at his belt and his entire teeth were pure gold.

"Hello," said Benedict. Suddenly he ripped the sword from the soldier's belt and in one swift strike, cut open his chest. The horrified soldier dropped dead to the floor. He bent down and picked out the soldier's gun and tossed it over to the professor. Then he looked forward and surveyed the scene in front of him.

Over thirty Omegans had dropped down on all sides of them and were fighting – or rather, killing the Epsilons.

Dr Macintyre had his own sword drawn and was cutting open Omegans single-handedly, left, right and centre. Commander Collington was standing beside him with his pistol drawn. The Minuet was poised a fair distance away from them with his royal sword stuck in the stomach of a fat Omegan. Blood was gurgling out of his belly and his mouth.

Suddenly an Omegan came for Benedict. Rolling up his lip, he turned round to face the soldier who was also carrying one of these golden swords.

"What d'you think you're doing with that?" sneered the Omegan. "They're ours – get your own."

"Oh, fuck off!" retorted Benedict, slashing forward with the blade. The enemy blocked the blow. He tried again, but again the soldier fought off the blade.

"What's the matter?" laughed the soldier. "Can't use a sword?"

"Not exactly," replied Benedict, taking out his pistol. "But I can use a gun."

"That's cheating – "

Benedict shot the man straight through the head.

"Help me!" a voice cried.

The commander turned to see the Minuet being restrained by two Omegan soldiers. A third soldier came up behind them – if you could call her a soldier.

She was a tall woman who wore the Omegan uniform, but without the sleeves. She carried a large sword at her belt and three knives.

"Help me!" cried the Minuet. "Benedict!"

The commander was already hurrying across to the scene. But he was too late, because the woman had already drawn her large sword. With blinding accuracy, she thrust it through his back. The Minuet screamed in absolute terror as the bloody blade shot out through his chest. Blood poured onto the white floor. The woman retracted the blade and then began slashing down again and again at the dying royal figure.

Benedict rushed over. The two soldiers who'd restrained the Minuet looked up in terror as the commander leapt into the air over them and struck down, severing open their throats. Both of them choked on their own filthy blood and collapsed feverishly to the floor.

The woman was angry. She raised her magnificent golden sword, trying to frighten Benedict, and in an instant she struck down. The commander only just managed to block the blow and had no time to manoeuvre.

The female soldier threw herself on top of him. She flattened the commander to the ground and knelt on his legs. Lowering the point of the sword to his chest, she smiled sadistically. Suddenly, Benedict threw the flat of his hand into her teeth. The surprise of which caused her to reel off him. He got up off the ground.

"I'll kill you for that, you imbecile!" cried the woman, picking herself off the floor.

Benedict suddenly leapt forward and kicked her in the face. The woman fell backwards with a yelp of surprise. But then she picked herself up for the second time, blood streaming down her nose.

"You fucker!" screamed the woman.

Benedict picked up his new golden sword, but to his dismay, he found that it was bent. However did that woman get a sword strong enough to bend another? He drew his gun and pointed it at the woman, but suddenly she struck it out of his hand.

"You bitch!" he cried. Quickly, he drew back his fist and then threw it as hard as he could into her jaw. A jet of blood spurted sideways.

She grabbed him by his collar and tried to throttle him. Benedict then shot his foot into her abdomen. She leapt back in slight pain, but not much.

Benedict made the stupid mistake of trying to locate his pistol. She caught him off guard and threw him backwards. He landed on his back; pain shot up his muscle. He shuffled back as she approached him. He frantically searched about for his gun. He couldn't find it anywhere. Then he backed into something. At first he thought it was his pistol, but as he reached for it, he realised that it was the Minuet's sword.

"Aha!" he cried pulling up the blade.

The woman began running at him, one of her knives drawn. Benedict whipped round and swung it as hard as he could into her side.

Both of them fell silent. He levered the blade out of her, realising he had cut half of her open.

She fell like a landslide to the ground.

Benedict stood there, a terrible feeling of guilt crossing onto his face. He had killed a woman. Yes, she *had* killed the Minuet most brutally, but to kill her in response? No, he shouldn't have done that. Even in this brutal world, there should've been *some* mercy.

He threw away the sword in disgust. His gun was lying only a few feet away from him. He picked it up off the ground and rushed back into the fight.

The Epsilons were losing the battle. No matter how much Dr Macintyre lunged forward with his sword; no matter how many bullets Commander Collington fired; no matter how much Bristol kicked and punched, the Epsilon Brotherhood were dropping like flies.

Benedict could see this. He lashed out with his gun and took down five men instantly; but then the Omega Brotherhood fought back even harder.

Commander Collington came over to him. "Benedict, we're losing this battle! We can't do a damn thing to shake them off, commander. They outnumber us three to one!"

"Keep fighting!" cried Benedict. "Keep – "

"Sir, we should surrender!"

"Do you think they'll take prisoners?" Benedict threw himself at three men, elbowing them all.

"Commander!" gasped Collington. He shot at one of them, catching him in the head.

Benedict shot the second one in the chest, the blast knocking them both backwards. The third one tried to restrain the commander. Benedict landed a punch in his stomach, then kicked him in the abdomen. It knocked him out.

Benedict saw that Bristol had been captured. She and several other soldiers were pinned to the floor, Omega soldiers guarding them. Dr Macintyre had managed to get out of the way: he had rushed over next to Commander Collington. Suddenly there was a cry as Professor Bentley was restrained. He swore angrily at his captors as they forced him to the floor.

Only Benedict, Collington, the good doctor and five soldiers were left standing – they had been driven into a tight circle. The soldiers guarding the prisoners seemed to be laughing at the remaining fighters.

"Give them hell," Benedict told his friends as he shot an oncoming attacker.

Suddenly, there was the sound of blood being spilt. Benedict risked a glance to see that four of the five soldiers had been slaughtered.

"Fuck," said Collington. In rage, he fired more bullets into the oncoming crowd of Omegans. Blood splattered all over his face.

"Commander Nettlefold!" cried the remaining soldier.

Benedict just managed to see him dragged by his neck into the armada. An Omegan raised his sword and struck down, slicing down into his face. Blood flew into the air.

Dr Macintyre struck forward and stabbed into the crowd. More blood was spilt. The raging medic cut and cut and cut and cut. Even more blood was spilt.

Commander Collington fired the last of his bullets. Exhausted, he drew his sword and flung himself into the danger.

As for Benedict: he stood a true soldier spraying bullets into the enemy. He cried out in anger when his barrel was finished. Hurriedly he began to reload, kicking an oncoming attacker in the chest. He yelled to Collington: "Cover me!"

The young commander began cutting down enemies in front of Benedict.

The commander finished reloading.

An enemy soldier jumped for him.

Benedict rolled over to one side and shot him through the neck. Blood flew into the air. The commander leapt up, just in time to see Collington wrestled to the ground.

Now only he and Dr Macintyre were still standing. The medic was ploughing his way into the armada, a path of dead bodies behind him. Blood was shooting itself everywhere.

Macintyre was then seized by three enemy privates. The medic was still flinging his sword everywhere, managing to cut down a sergeant, but his three captors jostled the sword from his hand and kicked it a good distance away from him.

Benedict was the last man standing.

He had managed to reload his gun one last time.

With his last bullets.

And he shot them out wide, taking down eight more of the enemy. The second he'd shot his last bullet, he realised that he was finished. He couldn't kill another man. He lowered his gun, placed it in his holster and raised his arms.

He was pushed to the floor and struck hard on the head with a club.

Benedict awoke to the feeling of a damp cloth being pressed against his skull. A young Asian girl of about twenty was hovering above him. She cradled his neck briefly and shoved a pillow under his head.

"Gentle," she whispered, placing a glass of water underneath his lips.

Imagine what a young girl would have thought of this man? What would she think of this rugged commander with a stubbed moustache and beard? How would she view this mentally scarred commander with tight fists and the dirty black hair? How *could* she view him…?

"You must drink," she whispered to Benedict. "Please…"

The commander groaned. He felt the young girl pouring the water slowly against his lips. Suddenly his hand shot up and grabbed the glass off her. In one second he had downed the lot.

The girl was shocked as this commander jumped up off the floor. He hadn't even noticed her yet. Benedict turned down to the timid young girl – the one who'd saved him.

"Well darling," he said to her, "if you're going to give me some water, give me the whole damn lot, not just dribbles!"

He looked around him. He was still in the valley, but now there were over two hundred Omegans scattered around. They'd set up tents throughout the battle scene. The dead had been carried away and wrapped in plastic sheets.

Benedict wandered away from the Asian girl. He trudged past Omegans, all of whom were busy with tent construction or were wrapping up the dead bodies in these plastic sheets.

He felt a hand on his shoulder. It wasn't a hand of sympathy of any kind, but a hand of restraint. He turned around to see a tall major with an orange face and dark brown hair. There was a great big victorious grin on his face.

"Who the hell are you?" said Benedict, grimacing back. "Where are all the Epsilons?"

"Over there," said the major, grinning even more. He pointed to what the commander first thought was a dishevelled tent – but as he gazed closer, he realised that it was a pile of bodies: all the Epsilon soldiers. Before he knew what was happening, he was running towards it. Frantically, he looked for Bristol's brown robes, Dr Macintyre's tank top Commander Collington's uniform, or Professor Bentley's neckerchief.

"Where are the others?" said Benedict. "What the fuck have you done with my friends?"

The major sighed. "I'm afraid, my dear friend, that all your soldiers had to be killed – to prevent uprising. However, your leaders have been put that tent over there," he informed, indicating a large brown shelter a fair distance away from them.

"I want to see them," said Benedict forcefully. "I want to see them now."

"Well before you start ordering me around like that," said the major, "let's get introductions out the way." He held out his hand to Benedict. "I am Major Thorbes Regan."

"I'm Commander Nettlefold," said Benedict, shaking the hand.

"Do you mean the famous Benedict!" shouted Regan gleefully. "Ah it is you! Brilliant! I have heard much about you, Commander! Much indeed! The man who put down - "

"I'm not interested in hearing about my heroics, major," said Benedict. "I want to see my companions."

"Why of course!" replied Major Regan. "I can grant you that request, indeed! Follow…"

Benedict followed the major to the tent. Regan opened the flap for him. The commander ducked as he entered, smiling when he recognised all three people on the floor.

Commander Collington lay heavily bruised and unconscious but alive on a small rug; Chief Inspector Bristol was having her cut arm being cared for by another Asian girl; but as for Professor Bentley, he was in deep conversation with one of the soldiers. His eyes lit up when he saw the commander.

"Dr Bentley!" cried Benedict, gripping the man by the shoulders. But then his heart slowed when the realisation came to him: where was Dr Macintyre?

"Where's the doctor?" said Benedict.

"I don't know, Commander," said the professor. "I was taken to this tent with Bristol and Collington – but Macintyre wasn't here."

Benedict said to Major Regan: "Where's Dr Macintyre?"

"Ah," replied Regan, "he's been taken somewhere special – come with me." The major led him out of the tent, across the busy ground and to a majestic-looking circus tent with spirals drawn on all sides, a spike on the roof and two oddly dressed Chinese guards standing by the entrance.

"What's this place?" Benedict enquired. "Why the Chinese guards?"

"Ah, this is our ambassadorial tent," said Regan. "Whenever we receive special guests on expeditions, we like to give them a welcome they'll never forget."

Now Benedict was truly sickened: even in the enemy's hands, Dr Macintyre *always* managed to escape the worst.

This was confirmed, when the commander was shown into the tent: the good doctor was relaxing in a Jacuzzi with twelve Chinese girls sitting on all sides of him. When he saw Benedict, his eyes opened fully and a smile came on his face.

"Benedict!" he exclaimed. "Oh, Commander! Please join me!"

"Well, I'll leave you to it," said Major Regan. "Do not fear; the water isn't contaminated with mind-controlling chemicals. Relax and enjoy yourself." With that, the officer left the tent. He heard him whisper something to the guards outside and walk off.

"Dr Macintyre," said Benedict, bending down next to the medic, "get your clothes back on. We need to talk."

"We can," retorted the doctor. "These girls don't speak a word of English. Come on, Benedict."

"Just get your clothes back on, and then we can talk, alright?"

"Oh for God's sake, Commander Nettlefold!" exclaimed Dr Macintyre. "Get in, mate! The water's lovely and warm!"

Benedict hated the medic more than ever now. He stood up straight before him and shouted:

"You unfeeling tosser! All the soldiers are dead! They've been butchered like pigs. They're piled up outside in a fucking heap – go an' see them if you don't believe me! Commander Collington's been knocked unconscious; Bristol's hurt so badly. You don't know what they're going to do to them yet! And all you can think of is a quick shag…"

"Excuse me – "

"Oh sorry, you're too shagged out with Adeline."

"Alright!" barked the medic. He waved his hand roughly and the Chinese girls got themselves out of the Jacuzzi and vanished out of the hut.

"We can talk now?"

"Yes, but I ain't getting out of the water."

"Okay, I can see that," replied Benedict. He took off his jumpsuit boots, seeing that his shoes were still in good shape – but as for the boots, they were a different matter: they'd been worn out completely: just tatters were left. He took off his uniform and shoes, and then joined Dr Macintyre in the Jacuzzi.

"It's alright, isn't it?" said Dr Macintyre. "Let the water sooth you, Commander."

"It *is* grand," smiled Benedict weakly. "But we need to talk about escape."

"Yes, I suppose we do," answered the medic. "But can't we first enjoy this splendid array of hospitality?"

"There's no time for that, doctor," said Benedict. "Has it occurred to you that they may be trying to make us feel homely, in order so they can prevent an uprising?"

"An uprising started by the five of us?"

"They were probably trying to accommodate us *while* they killed our surviving soldiers," Benedict said through gritted teeth.

"It's a possible theorem," replied Dr Macintyre. "But I'm not a physicist, nor a mathematician – I'm a doctor. Besides, it's not my problem to deal with – *you're* the soldier here, mate."

"Don't you dare say that, Dr Macintyre!" shouted Benedict. "Don't you ever fucking say that! Of course it's you're problem – they'll kill us all eventually…"

"You're being too outlandish," said the medic. "Don't worry, Benedict, if they wanted us dead, we'd be dead already."

"If you had actually listened to me," hissed Benedict, "then perhaps - "

Suddenly Major Regan barged back into the tent. Sweat was streaming down his face as he hurried over.

Benedict's heart leapt when he thought that they were being dragged out for execution – but the major merely shouted at them:

"Get out, both of you! Put your clothes back on! We're under attack! Hurry – quickly!"

Benedict leapt out the pool and threw his uniform back on. He found it much easier to walk with only his shoes on, but he still found it strenuous to do so.

Dr Macintyre was close behind him, still tying his new bowtie.

They went over to Major Regan who was loading his gun. "The two Chinese guards will take you to the tent where your companions are," he informed them. "Go!" he shouted.

Benedict and Dr Macintyre ran out the tent. The two Chinese guards were quick behind them.

Gunshots were ringing out as masked attackers fired upon the camp. The two Chinese guards instructed them to remain low. Both of them still had their sabres in their scabbards.

Suddenly fiery ripples exploded through the encampment as fire bombs were dropped. Omegans screamed in terror as their flesh was burnt of their skeletons. One man was unlucky enough to have one of the missiles strike him in the face. The headless burning corpse fell to the ground.

A bullet streamed past Benedict, catching one of the Chinese guards in the skull.

The other guard turned to them and shouted: "Behind the pile of corpses! Now!"

The commander and the medic threw themselves behind a pile of plastic corpses. The Chinese guard was quick to join them.

Benedict risked a glance round the plastic to see a few of the enemy. He saw that they wore black uniforms, same as them; but on their chests were the Lambda symbols. No! No, it couldn't be! It just couldn't be! Benedict squinted his eyes, but sure enough, the Lambda symbol was fixed on their chests.

Fresh encouragement filled him. Suddenly he snatched the sabre from the Chinese guard and plunged it into his side. Blood erupted onto the floor.

"Why did you do that?" gasped Macintyre. "Now they'll have us executed for sure!"

"Not necessarily, Dr Macintyre." Benedict pointed to an object in the sky. It was a bright red hot air balloon, and on-board, fleeing for his life, was Major Regan.

The Lambda Brotherhood was finishing off the last of the Omegans. A few of them had managed to flee into the void of the valley, and were being pursued and gradually slaughtered.

Benedict stood up and made his way over to one of the attackers. The Lambda soldier instantly took out his gun and pointed it at the commander, but when Benedict showed him the Epsilon symbol on him arm, the soldier lowered his weapon.

"Who are you?" the Lambda asked them.

"My name is Benedict Nettlefold – I'm a commander in the Epsilon Brotherhood. May I see your leader, if he is around?"

"Certainly," said the soldier. "But this associate of yours," he continued, pointing at Macintyre, "is to remain in the tent where we discovered the other captives."

"Of course," said Benedict. "Dr Macintyre, go to the captive tent." Benedict pointed at it. "It's that one there."

"But – "

"Just do as the soldier has asked!" shouted Benedict. "Go!"

The disgruntled medic trotted off.

"Follow me," said the Lambda soldier. He led Benedict to a group of three men. One of them ordered the other two to go upon seeing the Epsilon.

"Hello there!" said this man, reaching out his hand, nodding the escort to be dismissed. "I am Gene Simone, captain off the Lambda ship *Deviant*."

"I'm Benedict Nettlefold, a commander," replied the individual before him, in a manner that reflected his surprise, nervousness, and joy. "How did the Lambda Brotherhood survive? I thought that they were all killed off…"

"Oh, we survived!" said Captain Simone. "We're pride, you know. There's pride in the name, dear boy, pride in the name."

"I trust that all my friends are not assumed to be Omegans," said Benedict, obviously not getting a clear reply out of Simone.

"No, not at all!" replied Captain Simone. "Just you understand that your friends will be cared for upon the *Deviant*!"

"What's the *Deviant*?"

"You'll see, Benedict!" said Simone. "Here she is!"

No, the *Levitator* and the *Champion* weren't the only super ships in the fleet. Through the dim clouds above came a massive shape: it was another one of these majestic ships. She was a beauty in her own style. She opened her landing struts and descended to the ground a fair distance from the encampment, settling down with a massive hiss.

Chapter 9   Let's Fly Away

As they flew over the vast land of Pacifica, the relieved companions half slept, half talked. Captain Simone had their clothes taken away and sent them to be washed. They had been given bathrobes instead and sent to rest in the lounge while maids set up their quarters.

Benedict downed the last of a well-earned glass of vodka, putting the glass on the small table beside him. He rubbed his forehead, feeling the stress come away from him. He glanced across at his friends: Dr Macintyre had dozed off on an armchair; Professor Bentley was stretched out on a sofa reading a scientific journal; Commander Collington was drinking a glass of bold whiskey; and as for Bristol, she was fast asleep on a sofa adjacent to him.

His hand reached down to his belt, making sure his gun was secure. Just before they had left, Captain Simone had sent some men to retrieve their weapons. He trusted Benedict with his gun, but the Lambda captain was unsure of why a commander such as himself would keep his weapon on him at all times…

Benedict reached into his robe and removed his pipe. Since leaving on this mission, he had kept his pipe and a pouch of tobacco on him at all times. Carefully, he emptied the powder into the pipe and lit it. His whole body seemed to relax as the smoke entered his mouth and infiltrated his muscles.

Suddenly there was another striking sound a few feet away. Commander Collington had lit his own pipe and was drawing in the cloud.

"You're too young to do that," remarked Benedict.

Collington was irritated at this: "Excuse me, commander, but you're my age too."

"Yes, but at least you have long adventurous years ahead of you, hopefully with a wife and children."

"What do you think Captain Simone's going to do?" enquired Commander Collington, obviously trying to change the subject.

"Probably the same as we set out to do," replied Benedict. "I should think so, anyway; he seemed pretty intent on wiping out all the Omegans in Streak Valley."

"Sure he did – but he might not want to attack the stronghold."

"Even if he doesn't, he might give us some Lambdas, you know…"

"Hmm, he might."

Benedict sighed. "We'll have to talk it over with him."

Commander Collington bowed his head slightly, drawing another breath from his pipe.

Benedict glanced over to Bristol; she had half fallen off the sofa. He reached out his hand and pushed her back on. Thankfully, she still retained herself in sleep.

Commander Collington continued to smoke his pipe. He turned to Benedict and said: "What are you going to do once this is all over?"

Benedict shrugged: "I suppose I'll be returning to my policing job. The cops will probably have a heap of tasks for me to do, so I won't be bored stiff."

"Alright then," said Collington. "But I thought they were going to make you general after this; you said you've always wanted it."

"I'd love that position, Commander," said Benedict, "but when I was offered that position, I was ruined. Being offered that position sounds great, but it won't be the same, not without Adeline at my side, commander. To be honest, I love doing these menial jobs. I love going to these pubs to take out criminal gangs and arrest drunks. Believe me, commander, I have this menial job; but it keeps me out of these social dangers."

"There's no such thing as a social danger," said Collington.

"Yes, there is – you just don't notice them."

Captain Simone entered the lounge. He spotted Benedict and came right over. "Ah, there you are, commander!" he said. "Your quarters are all ready."

Professor Bentley sat right up. "They are?!" he exclaimed. "Brilliant!"

Dr Macintyre woke up at the same moment, running a hand through his hair. "About time too," he grumbled.

"Here's your key," said Simone, handing it over to the medic. Macintyre took it and vanished out of the lounge.

"Smug git," Benedict whispered in the direction of Dr Macintyre. "Lazy little tosser."

Captain Simone paused for a second before handing out the other keys. "Oh, I see," he remarked when he saw Bristol fast asleep. "Benedict, your quarters are next to hers. See, if you can carry her, then – "

"Commander Collington will take her," said Benedict. "Right, let's go."

Benedict's quarters were located just down the hallway. Shrugging chillily, he opened Bristol's door. Collington carried the detective in and placed her gently on the bunk.

"Right," said Collington as he came out, "I'll be off."

"See ya then," Benedict replied. He opened his door and trudged inside.

The quarters were the same as on the *Levitator*, except that there weren't three guards in there waiting to kill him. All that was in there was his bunk, a table, and his uniform all cleaned.

"Glad to be out of this shit," he said, taking off his robe. He threw his uniform back on, feeling its soothing texture rub into his skin, the tightness of the waist clench his sides, and, when he put his gun belt back on, the feeling of the rubber massage his waist.

He sat on his bed and did up the shoes. They'd been polished quite finely, so they sent a black glitter around the room. He finished his pipe and put the remnants in the waste bin.

That was when Bristol came in. She entered without knocking and sat like an empress on the desk chair. She didn't even give the commander time to react – she jumped straight into the question.

"Why did you do it?"

"Do what?" Benedict asked, quite infuriated at this. "Look, I didn't carry you to your quarters; Mr Collington did, alright?"

"I'm not talking about that," said Bristol, "I'm talking about the battlefield. When you killed that woman."

"Look, she killed the Minuet and tried to kill me!" shouted Benedict. "What was I supposed to do, hmm? Make peace with her? She was trying to fucking kill me!"

"The *way* you killed her!" screamed Bristol. "You hurt her so badly. I saw you."

"How long have you been a detective, Miss Bristol?" said Benedict.

"This is my debut mission," she replied.

"Well you don't know the first darn thing about killing, if I may say so," Benedict stated. "You don't know anything about war. In war, *people die*!" The last sentence was said so loud that the buzz hung around in the wall for several seconds.

"That wasn't war back then, Benedict; that was murder. Something only you can do, Commander."

"Excuse me – "

"May I say something?"

"Go ahead!"

Bristol stood up from the chair, towering over the commander. She looked him in the eye and said clearly: "You scare me, Benedict."

Benedict would have vociferated loudly at this, but instead he remained silent.

Bristol continued. "I thought that you, as an officer, would have some respect for a young woman like me, but no; all you want is the sex."

Benedict sat silent and sullen as she walked out the door.

"Damn them all," said Benedict as he lay back on his bunk. "Damn Macintyre, damn Bristol, damn the whole fucking lot."

Later that evening, Commander Collington came by to Benedict's quarters, telling him that Captain Simone had invited them all to dinner in his lounge.

"There's a suit for you done by the tailor," Collington informed, indicating a package in his hand. "He sent it for you."

"Thanks, Justin," said Benedict, taking the package from him.

"Are you all right?" Collington asked.

"I'm fine," said Benedict.

"There's something else as well," said Collington. "Captain Simone insisted on you taking a date to the dinner."

"I don't think there's the time," said Benedict. "I've got things to do."

"You don't have to find one, Commander, your date is here with me."

"Excuse me?" remarked Benedict, but he'd hardly the time to finish, because she approached him from behind Collington. He couldn't help but admire her beauty: the blond hair, the blue eyes, the faintly tanned skin. He reached out his hand and shook hers. "Benedict Nettlefold," he introduced himself to her.

"Vanessa," she replied weakly. "I will see you later." She winked shyly at him, then vanished down the corridor

"What time's dinner?" Benedict asked, watching her uniform disappear round the corner.

"Eight."

"Alright. I'll see you then."

"Right." Commander Collington headed off for his own quarters.

Benedict opened the paper casket in his quarters, discovering the suit to be a standard shirt and bowtie. He changed into it, keeping an eye on the time. When it was time to go, he grabbed his pipe and tobacco, and then made his way to the lounge.

It had changed from before. The sofas and armchairs had been moved out of the way, making room for a long table with goblets, plates and silver cutlery to be set up.

Captain Simone was sitting at the head of the table talking with his senior officers. He smiled when he saw Benedict and invited him to sit down. He introduced the commander to his officers.

Professor Bentley and Commander Collington entered, deep in conversation and fresh black suits. They sat down next to Benedict and poured themselves some wine.

Dr Macintyre entered next. He wasn't wearing a black suit, but instead he wore a fine frilly shirt with tassels on the sleeves and a tank top. He sat down opposite to Benedict, seeming impatient for the service to begin.

Benedict kept glancing at the empty seat across from him. His date's.

And suddenly she came in. Fucking gorgeous she was. A velvety emerald dress hung from her shoulders, her hair was combed back and knotted in a loose bun, and her jewelled eyes glittered.

Benedict just sat there, quite puzzled: what was he supposed to do next?

"You're meant to take her by the hand and lead her to the table," Commander Collington whispered in his ear. "She's your date, remember…?"

"Oh," stuttered Benedict. He approached the girl and kissed her on the hand. He escorted her to the table and pulled back the chair for her. Satisfied she was comfortable, he returned to his own seat.

"Where's Bristol?" enquired Commander Collington. "She was having a dress fitted, but she *shouldn't* take this long…"

But his puzzlement was answered.

She was more beautiful than ever. She wore a velvety red dress with jewels on the neckpiece. Her eyelashes were coated with dark makeup. She wore a ruby necklace with faint glimmers of emeralds in the golden chain.

She was beautiful.

"Ah, Miss Bristol!" said Captain Simone, running forward to greet her. He kissed her hand lightly. "Well," he glued, "I am thoroughly pleased to welcome you to dinner, my dear. I shall introduce you first to my arms officer, Lieutenant Paul."

Benedict had half expected one of the senior officers to stand up, but instead this young man with frizzy blond hair rose up from the table. Benedict hadn't noticed him at first, but there he was. Bristol seemed to take to him and him to her.

Dinner was served: a selection of fine roast, wine and bread. The other officers seemed to be thoroughly enjoying their meals, the whole host of tastes available to them. Benedict talked for a bit with the navigation officer sitting next to him, but apart from that, he was bored stiff. He glanced across to his date from time to time. He talked with her a bit, but he didn't know how to treat a woman on a date.

He kept glancing down the table to where Bristol and Mr Paul were talking deeply. They seemed to be enjoying each other's company and *he* touched her on the shoulder every ten seconds.

Benedict shivered slightly. Not a chill shiver that he felt earlier, but a shiver of being uncomfortable. This was only the fourth time he had been to a formal occasion in his life (the previous time was at the academy when he went the king's banquets). And with a date! He didn't feel right. Not because of her specifically. It was the formality that got to him. He wasn't used to it. He didn't know it.

No, Benedict was used to eating dinner at home on his own or on battlefields. Perhaps with John when they visited each other. You see, ever since Dr Macintyre ruined his wedding, Benedict had been plunged into this world of solitary meals, lonely nights and lovesickness.

But in those long days, loneliness had become a friend to him. It hurt him so much, but at least it never left him.

And now sitting with Vanessa on this 'date' made him feel uncomfortable. He wasn't used to the feeling of having a woman there who was there for *him*. He just wasn't used to it.

Benedict was never meant for these occasions.

Dinner passed briefly but in such a long time. Dessert was a piece of chocolate cake, nothing special – for him anyway. But the wine was splendid! It was soothing, much better than the stuff he had at home. Benedict considered asking Simone if he could take a bottle home with him.

When the dessert was finished, Captain Simone made a brief speech welcoming the companions, and then bade them all goodnight.

As Benedict rose out of his seat, he saw Vanessa rise up to greet him. His heart was thumping out of his chest, but he didn't know what to do with it. The date in front of him was just a woman. Not a woman who was there for him.

But he thought he'd better do it anyway.

"Listen, love," he said to her, "do you want to go to my quarters?"

"I'd love to," she said, "but I feel really tired. I need to go to bed. I'm sorry, Commander."

"It's all right," said Benedict. "I'd best be getting to bed anyway myself."

Benedict walked out of the lounge. He bade Macintyre, Bentley and Collington a decent evening, and then trudged back to his quarters.

On the way, he passed several drunken officers falling about the place. They'd had too much of that wine. Benedict was accustomed to the alcohol, but they weren't. The commander *had* to laugh at them as they hopelessly tried to find their cabins.

But his smile was wiped clean off his face when he approached his cabin. Bristol and this young officer were going into her cabin, together.

"Oh fuck," he remarked as their door closed. "I'm not going to get an inch of sleep." He turned the other way and explored the rest of the ship.

It wasn't much different from the *Levitator*, but there was a difference all the same: a difference of atmosphere. He made his way up to the command deck. No resistance was made to his entry as he sat down in the captain's chair. The two pilots were too busy trying to fly the ship through a storm they were in.

Without warning, sleep took him. He began dreaming.

"Sir," one of them said, "we're passing through the dense part of the storm. Can you give us a heading?"

"I'm not Captain Simone," replied Benedict sullenly. "It's Commander Nettlefold. I just came up here to have a look."

"No, sir, you are. Please give us a heading."

"You're the pilots – you tell me what heading. And I'm not your captain."

"But you are, sir - "

"I said I'm not your captain!" Benedict screamed loudly. "Okay?"

"Sir, we need a heading." Suddenly the screen shattered. The rush of air howled. The two screaming pilots were sucked out.

Benedict breathed in deeply. "Shit!" he shouted. "Help! Please help!"

The intercom came on. Simone was speaking. "Ladies and gentlemen, we are going to crash, I repeat, we are going to crash. It's all Benedict's fault; he can't do anything. Blame him. He's incredibly useless."

Then the fire ripped through the ship, engulfing Benedict. He screamed like an animal as the Deviant exploded into fragments.

"Commander!" someone was screaming. "Commander, wake up!"

Benedict was shaken up from his dream. He sat shivering on the captain's chair, sweat pouring on his forehead.

"What happened?" he enquired.

"You fell asleep," said the pilot. "God, you were shaking like a hydrogen bomb! Should I inform Captain Simone?"

"No, it's all right," said Benedict. "I'll head back to my quarters." He rose up out of the chair and walked back down the corridor. He opened his door and fell onto his bed.

He could hear the noises next door. Bristol was obviously having the time of her life. They seemed to be really going for it...

"Shit," muttered Benedict. He shut his eyes, thinking about his adventure so far.

Indeed it had been interesting, adventurous, but like everything else, it had taken its steady toll.

He was just about to drift off to sleep when there was a knock on his door. He investigated and found that Vanessa was outside – still wearing her remarkable emerald dress.

"I've changed my mind," she whispered, shutting the door behind her.

"About what?"

She undid the straps on her dress and let it fall to the floor in front of her.

She wasn't much, Benedict thought. But he'd better fuck her anyway – since she was here. He undid his bowtie and barely removed his jacket before she leapt onto him, burying his face in her chest.

The sex wasn't as good as he'd anticipated. It was more forced than enjoyable. Of course, she was gorgeous, but she just lay flat on the bed, letting him make all the moves. She didn't even scream; instead she just huffed and puffed, whispering in his ear: "Try harder, Benedict. I'm not a fucking tourist."

"*You* try harder," he shot back.

When they'd finished, Vanessa just got out of the bed and put her dress back on. She didn't even say goodbye.

And like all the other one night stands, Benedict was left lying in bed, so lonely. And no one gave a damn about him.

Chapter 10   Realisation

If ever there was a time in which the tough Major Regan became the infidel, it was now. Being one who never liked to let down his Lord Marius, Regan found what he had to announce very difficult indeed. Right at that moment as he stood outside the chamber door, the major wished he was on holiday somewhere – perhaps in Lincolnshire, far away from the tropics.

The ticking clock behind him reminded him that he had less than a minute before he went in. He sucked in his stomach as he breathed deeply in.

The door opened and the major wandered straight in. The sunny chamber greeted him like an incredible omen. This was the chamber in the front of the fortress. This was the room in which Lord Marius and Professor Davenport liked to receive good news, especially progressive news.

Major Regan marched over to where Lord Marius was set back in his armchair. As for the professor, he was sitting on the adjacent sofa. In his arms was a scientific journal. He glanced up at the major as he stood before Lord Marius.

"Yes, Major?" asked Lord Marius eagerly. "Good news I hope? The infidels that are the Epsilons are dead?"

"No, my lord," replied Major Regan. "I regretfully tell you this."

"How?" Lord Marius bellowed. "How did those *cunts* get away?!"

"My lord," said Regan, sweat pouring down his forehead. "I apologise, but we were attacked."

"By whom?"

"The Lambda Brotherhood," informed Major Regan. "They outnumbered us, ten to one, sir. They attacked the encampment and left once they had retrieved the prisoners in one of these new hover ships the Epsilons have built."

"Firstly," said Lord Marius, "the Lambda Brotherhood is extinct! They killed themselves off with that bio accident, or whatever. And secondly, we are not just an army: we are the supreme Omega Brotherhood! There could be ten of us and a hundred of them, and we should still win the day! You do not seem to understand this, do you? Or maybe I should get someone else to lead the troops… And thirdly, Mr Regan, there are only two prototypes of these new ships in this world: the one that you shot down and the *Champion* back on their territory. However, there *will* soon be three: we shall build one. It will be the strongest, mightiest fucking ship on the planet. I'll arm it with super bio weapons, nerve toxin, and big fucking nuclear warheads!"

"Indeed, sir," said Major Regan. "May I point out, my lord that the ship is real; I saw it with my own eyes."

"Alright, I believe you," snapped Lord Marius. "Just tell me where they're headed."

"I am not certain, my lord," said Regan, "but if they are going to launch some sort of attack on us, they'll need to regroup and refuel. My best guess is they'll stop at the city of Sir Finley, a major fuel depot far inland from the coast, towards the south of Pacifica."

"Alright, I know where it is!" said Lord Marius angrily. "How certain are you?"

"It's my best guess, sir."

"Very well; I want you to take an aerial squad of fifteen slaughterers and attack them when they land at Sir Finley. I want every one of them, Lambdas included, killed! Is that understood?"

"Yes, my lord."

"Then get on with it, right now. Dismissed."

"Yes, my lord." Major Regan turned smartly and disappeared out of the chamber. Relief passed through him when he was outside. At least Lord Marius had given him a second chance, but it had ruined his chance for a spot of leave.

He began to make his way to where the slaughterers were kept. On his way he passed his leading pilot, Captain Agathaninon, a short thin man with a small brown moustache. Regan took the captain to the side and said to him:

"Captain, ready fourteen of your pilots; Lord Marius has ordered us to go to Sir Finley for a little payback."

"Yes, sir," replied Captain Agathaninon, smiling deeply. "I'll go and get fourteen of my best men."

"Good," said Regan. "Meet me on the runway in half an hour."

"Yes, sir!"

And so it was like that. Their fate was sealed. They were about to fight a man who had lost so much in his life, that he cared not who he killed, injured, or hurt. And that half hour later when the slaughterers were lined up ready for takeoff, the pilots had no clue what was about to happen to them.

Major Regan was a pilot himself. He'd taken his own slaughterer out of its private hangar and lined up at the rear of the queue. He watched as Captain Agathaninon ripped off into the sky, hiking his way into the clouds. The others went next. Then finally it was the major's turn. He clipped on the flight peg and activated the thrusters. Soon he was speeding down the runway and then took off into the clouds.

Benedict was incredibly displeased with Captain Simone's ethos regarding the speed of the mission. Yes, the captain had the same ambition as himself (to bring down Lord Marius), but why the hell did he want to stop in Sir Finley?

"Captain, I checked your fuel content earlier," grumbled Benedict. "You've got more than enough to get there – and back!"

"My word is final, Commander," said Simone. "We are stopping for four hours in Sir Finley, so we can take on supplies. Look, Lord Marius is not going to have won the day if we're four hours late."

"Now that's where you're wrong, captain…"

Dr Macintyre, Commander Collington and Professor Bentley were sitting on the sofa behind the confrontation between Benedict and Captain Simone. Bristol was sitting on the lap of Lieutenant Paul who had settled himself on a cosy armchair.

"Commander," said Simone, "there's nothing you can do about it. We *are* stopping in Sir Finley. The crew needs to be fed and watered…"

"From what we had last night, I should think we've plenty enough."

"Excuse me, mister," said Captain Simone, "that's quite a ridiculous comment you've made there. I shall tell you that we *are* dwindling on supplies. Now, are you going to be my ally or not?"

"What kind of a fucking question is that?" snarled Benedict. "How fucking dare you speak to me like that! What do you think you are, hey? Some sort of motherfucking god?"

Captain Simone just stood there growling at the commander. He eyed him closely, trying to burn a mental message into his mind.

Benedict turned and shot out the room. He stomped his way up to an observation balcony located at the bow of the ship and stormed outside. The fresh air whipped around his neck, cooling off the sweat that had formed there. He took out a packet of cigarettes and flicked one of them to his lips. Lighting it, he leant on the banister and breathed in the smoke.

"Fucking idiot," he cursed. He examined the pack of fags, finding that they weren't the special ones made in the nearby village to where he lived, but city cigarettes. The things you buy from these rundown boozer shops that cell spirits, drugs, and toys (not children's ones though). On the front of the pack was an image of a poor old lady dying from an asthma attack. Underneath a piece of writing read: *Smoking has serious consequences.* Shrugging, he replaced the packet in his front pocket.

"Are you all right?" said someone behind him.

It was a sudden shock to him that made his heart leap. He turned around quite angrily and said: "Don't do that!"

"I'm sorry," said Bristol. "Listen – "

"I know what you're going to say, Miss Bristol," said Benedict. "I don't exactly want to know."

"You have it in for me, don't you?"

"No I don't!" snapped Benedict. "You're the one who's got it in for me! Ever since the crash when you found Tame totally fucked up and dead, you've constantly been having a go at me. I've been trying to help you, detective, but all you want to do is slag me off, and then fuck a young officer!"

"Oh I get it…" Bristol seemed furious at him now. Sweat – not tears – streamed down her cheeks. "You're just a jealous boy now, aren't you? You don't have any fucking respect for me at all! I've got problems – "

"You've got problems?" Benedict screamed. "Lady, the problems I've been faced with would blow your bloody head off!"

"No, the point is that I do have problems, but when I'm with Lieutenant Paul, they seem to evaporate." Bristol looked deeply at him. "When we're together, like last night when we had sex, my problems just faded. You might not believe this, commander, but when you climax with the one you love, you feel all the boundaries slip away. There's just you and your other half… together."

"Listen, Miss Bristol, I don't want to know anything about your filthy sex life. And to be honest, I don't give a shit…"

Bristol slapped him in the face at that moment. A tingling sensation that spread far from his cheek, down deep into his heart. It hurt. Very, very deeply.

"How dare you…" he spat at her. "You little fucking bitch." He smacked his hand across her face. "Don't you dare hit me, you fucking whore." He slashed his hand into her jaw. "What the fuck d'you think I am…?!" He crashed his hand into her cheek. "Motherfucker! I mean, are you trying to have sex with every bastard in fucking existence?!" He smacked her again. "*Bitch*!" he screamed, spittle flying out of his gritted teeth. Then suddenly he grasped her neck, squeezing tightly. "If you ever hit me again, I'll give you exactly what you want. I'll give you a nice little shag – but I'll make sure you never forget it."

He smacked her again, with clawed hands, digging his nails into her cheek and peeling open the flesh.

"I'm so *fucking* tired of life!" he screamed. "Enough! Enough! *Enough*!"

She whimpered as she felt the cut under her left ear. She looked up at him, deeply horrified. She hated and feared him. So much. So much. She began to cry, tears – not sweat – pouring down her cheeks.

"I'm sorry," he whispered, raising his hand and stroking away the blood. "Jesus Christ, I'm sorry." He touched her arm. "You were right, Rachel. I'm sorry."

She said nothing.

"I'll take you to your quarters," he said quietly, putting an arm round her. He led her slowly off the balcony.

When they reached her quarters, Bristol opened the door. Benedict led her inside and sat her down on her bed. He shut the door, and then tended to her injury. Indeed he had cuffed her hard, for the blood had spread down her face. Reaching out to examine it, she suddenly shoved him away.

"Let me take a look at it," he said, putting his hand out again. He went into the bathroom and soaked a tissue with water. He put it to her face and wiped away more of the blood. It was only a small cut, but even they can bleed so badly. He threw the tissue in the bin, and was about to get another one, but the cut had stopped bleeding.

"I'm sorry," she whispered. "I'm sorry."

"No, Miss Bristol, it's not you who should be apologising. It's - "

"No, not that," she said. "Before, when I said that you scared me; I didn't mean it. You did your duty in that battle, Benedict. I criticised you about it, but you killed that woman to protect the Epsilon Brotherhood, to protect home." She put her hand on his. "To protect me…"

"Why are you doing that?" enquired Benedict.

"You should know why," smiled the detective. She kissed him, plainly but fully.

Benedict was stunned. His heart stopped. Bristol had kissed him.

Would his own personal war end? Then and there?

"Rachel," he said, squeezing her hand, "what about Lieutenant Paul?"

"Benedict, when I slept with him, it wasn't that great. All the barriers faded, save one. I didn't *really* want to have sex with him."

"Rachel," he whispered, "I want you as well. But there's a problem. After what I've done to you, I don't know - "

She kissed him again, whispering in his ear: "Save the apologies for later."

Bristol shifted herself back from him and then undid her front, not hiding an inch. She removed her uniform and sat paralyzed in front of him. Kissing him for the third time, she groped around his waist.

Benedict seemed powerless to stop her. "I should report to Captain Simone," he whispered as she pulled off the last of his clothes.

"That can wait, Commander. Please, enjoy me…"

"Oh, fucking hell. Jesus Christ. I must be having a little bit too much fun…"

"What's wrong with that?" she smiled. "Come on, Benedict; come on, feel me here. In fact, wait. First…" She seemed to stutter not out of nervousness, but out of decision. "First," she whispered, removing her bra, "I need you to kiss me. Any way you want to. I need you to do that…"

He didn't catch the rest of what she said; he just stared at her front. He was quite turned on by the sight of her quite large breasts bulging out like the Himalayas. And they were tight and smooth, and they were beckoning him in. He sat at the end of the bed and she sat between his legs. He reached out his hand... and touched one of the mountains. He wanted to just stroke them ever so lightly, but she held his hands there, moaning and breathing out heavily. "Do it harder," she moaned. Again, he was quite powerless. He rubbed his hands up and down.

Saliva ran out of her mouth, dribbling down her jaw and onto his hands, forming a smooth layer between his hands and her breasts. And even more saliva drooled down her chin. And soon her entire front was covered in a wet, shiny layer.

She turned around without much warning and wrapped her legs around his waist and suddenly he was in her. She let out a great sigh that sounded throughout the room, and then she kissed him, taking his breath a trillion miles away.

"Rachel," he said quite suddenly, "I will not treat you like a whore. Holding you, I want to make love to you, but not like that. Like this."

He put his hand around her neck and lowered the detective to the pillow. He kissed her methodically, but passionately. He was coming away with her, discovering the girl whom he had secretly admired from the start. He held her against his hips, running his hands up her thighs, round her abdomen and up to her breasts. She winced slightly when he did this, but not out of pain, but sheer love and pleasure. He ran his hands back down to her hips, feeling how weak she was, feeling her smooth cream skin.

Suddenly she turned over and pushed Benedict on his back. It wasn't a hard push, but more of a gentle roll. He held her hair in one hand and lowered her head down to his with the other, kissing her gently. But she didn't. Any Tom, Dick or Harry could tell you she was doing it not to get pleasure but to express love.

And he returned that love by stroking her back ever so lightly. But *she* wasn't so light. She arched backwards, breathing heavily, groaning as she tightened every muscle in her body. Her muscles grimaced loudly in the pale moonlight as her face tensed. She continued to fall back, leaning so far that her breasts stuck into the air, covered in the bright light of the room.

Then suddenly it came. He gripped her tightly by the hips as his body joined with hers. She continued on top of him. She was expressing her love to him, completely oblivious to the fact that he had pretty much climaxed. She was trying to get everything out of him. Finally she realised that he was out and she slowed down. Eventually she came to a complete stop. She sat atop of him breathing at quick intervals.

Benedict let out a slight laugh, and soon they both were laughing out loud. A sense of sexual relief and love had come over them both.

Bristol wiped the sweat of her forehead and suddenly collapsed onto him.

She wasn't like the others. She seemed tiny against him. The others always set up an emotional barrier between them both. But Bristol was different. There was something in the way she'd held his face above hers. And unlike the others, she'd clung to him like a magnet.

And unlike the others, he had tried to be gentle with her. Well, he'd tried... He'd been caught between high... and low. He'd thought he'd better settle midway.

But the affection they shared! It was something they'd both never really felt before. Benedict was just discovering it, and he loved it.

Everything was peaceful. Everything. He was so relaxed and stable that later during the night, when he lay half awake, half asleep, he just stared at her. Her purple-tainted hair was flung smoothly against her shoulder. Her pale face was fast asleep on the pillow.

He put his arm around her and brought her close to him. Resting his head on the pillow, he found himself truly admiring her. She was just so incredibly beautiful.

But something was the matter. He wanted to love her, but he couldn't. A flashback came up of that doomed wedding. That was the last time he'd felt love. But then Dr

Macintyre had ruined it, destroyed his career, and threw away his future. On that long journey he'd undertaken to be together with Adeline and have his dream commission, it had all ended in him being a rapist.

How could he love again after that?

Some weeks ago, he'd craved the opportunity for a second chance. Now that second chance was here. He looked at Bristol, such a beautiful girl. She was the second chance in his life – the commission would come later.

But after what he had been through with Dr Macintyre, how *could* he love her? When they'd climaxed earlier, Benedict had enjoyed himself – thoroughly. He felt like a free man again, but now the notions of a rapist were coming back to him.

After having a charge like that, there was no way that Benedict could ever love her. He looked so closely at the girl next to him. He kissed her again, but lightly so as not to wake her. He got himself out of the bed and slowly put on his uniform.

Minutes later, he had vanished.

The next day, the city of Sir Finley came into view. At first it was a tiny glimmer of smoke in the distance, but an hour later it was a major bustle of activity before them.

All this was observed from the command deck. Captain Simone sat on his chair with the companions behind him. Benedict stood close to Bristol, but made sure that Dr Macintyre didn't see anything. The good doctor was busy talking things over with Commander Collington and Professor Bentley.

They had begun to pass over the city now; Benedict could just see the massive alleyways, busy as hell. He could see the distant markets, the townspeople bargaining with everything they could possibly think of.

The pilots carefully guided the ship over Sir Finley – when I say 'carefully', I mean they were trying to avoid the other air traffic. They were heading for a central tower in the city; other air traffic was hovering around it.

"What's the big spike for?" Benedict enquired.

"That's their air traffic control tower," explained Captain Simone. "We 'check-in' there and they tell us which alley to go to."

"Excuse me?"

Simone laughed. "Don't you understand, Commander? This city is one massive airport! These alleys I've mentioned are for zeppelins to land. All who live in them help load and refuel the ships, and sometimes accommodate the crews."

Benedict was impressed with amazement: entire communities dedicated to the welfare of passing ships – that was something they never taught at the academy…

One of the pilots was speaking to the tower. He acknowledged the instructions and then turned to Simone. "We've got clearance to land in Alley 6W."

"Very good," said Captain Simone. "Proceed."

The pilot adjusted the stick and turned the wheel slightly. The *Deviant* began to bank and then pick up speed. The pilot kept it slow though, not wanting to collide with any of the zeppelins and balloons parked above the alleyways. They directed themselves towards the western part of the city where Section 6 was located. They found their space in hardly anytime at all.

Benedict sighed – not in a frustrated manner though – when he saw all the children rush out of their houses to greet the travellers, admiring the weird new ship above them.

"Easy," whispered the pilot as he lowered the *Deviant* downwards. He grasped the stick loosely, changing down the settings. "Opening landing feet," he announced. The pilots worked together to descend the *Deviant* into the deep alley. Suddenly there was a gentle thud and the ship came to a stop.

But not the pilots. "Powering down engines," they announced. "Draining antigravity chamber. Opening main exit ramp…"

"Welcome to Sir Finley," said Captain Simone. "Let's go and meet the locals."

The party who descended down the ramp were both excited and nervous. It was the heat of the day here and the souls that greeted them off the ship weren't much different either. They carried heavy buckets of materials that must've weighed a tonne. Women rushed out to jostle their children back indoors. The strong men came forward with these heavy buckets and stopped before the companions. They were from Pacific tribes, and had obviously settled in this remarkable place many generations ago.

As Benedict descended down the ramp, he caught sight of this. His hand tightened on his gun.

"Hand off your weapon," whispered Captain Simone. "These people *are* friendly."

The commander looked over to Bristol, Collington, and Macintyre, seeing that they too were indeed agreeing with the captain. Benedict rested his hand in his pocket instead.

Captain Simone walked out to greet the gathered crowd. He raised his head, seeing if he could see the back end. He shrugged and then raised his voice: "Do you understand me?" he asked them. "We need refuelling. Refuelling – do you understand that? We need - "

"We understand," said a man coming forth from the audience. He was a dark man with his hair long and unclean. He eyed them with those dark sinister eyes. "We understand," he repeated. "We shall refuel your ship and we shall supply you with resources. Then we expect you to leave."

"Very well," said Captain Simone. "My men will remain in the ship, if that is your wish."

"We will begin," said the man.

"Good," said the captain. "Okay gentlemen, let's return to the ship."

It was a few hours later when Bristol came into his quarters. She seemed so sad, her eyes hung low in the dim light. She quickly brushed away a tear.

"Benedict," she whispered, "can I have a word with you?"

"Of course," said the commander. "We should be away in a few minutes, so – "

"Benedict, I want to talk to you about something else," Bristol said quietly. "It's about the other night."

"What about the other night?" he said. "I apologise about leaving your room when you were asleep – "

"It's not just that," said the detective. "It was the sex mainly."

"What about it?"

The detective seemed nervous about how to say this. "You weren't exactly... enjoying it."

"Of course I was!" laughed Benedict.

"What is it, Commander?" she said. "Is it because of Lieutenant Paul?"

"No!" snapped Benedict. "No way! It's just, Dr Macintyre..."

"Look, he wouldn't have barged in..."

"No," said Benedict. "You don't understand, detective. You really, really don't... When Dr Macintyre ruined my wedding those years ago, he left a permanent scar behind, Rachel. He hurt me so badly, that whenever I experience love, I think back to that conviction. I think back, and I can't fucking help it. It's damn well getting to me."

"Why?"

"Rachel," he said plainly, "as much as I love you, I can't. Do you know why? Dr Macintyre has ruined it for me. He turned me into the convicted rapist I am today. He fucking did it! Basically, I can't love you without realising the conviction that I've got. I'm sorry, Rachel. I am so fucking sorry."

"Please, Benedict," she whimpered. "I can't go on without you..."

"Well, you'll have to sweetheart; I'm sorry about it." Benedict took in a sharp intake of breath. "Here's it in simple terms, sweetie: When you get a twenty-something doctor, kick him in the fucking bollocks, he turns around, sees a simple man like me, makes up a rumour that I threatened to fuck someone against their will, and then I can't fucking love anyone. I'm sorry, my dearesy. Now, if you will excuse me, I have to fuck off somewhere else." He swirled around and marched stiffly down the corridor, hearing Rachel behind him scream: "Benedict!"

She screamed again: "Benedict!"

The commander turned back, expecting to see her running up to him. But he found himself confronted by Captain Simone. He was about to greet him, but then noticed the blood running down his lips. Suddenly, the captain was thrown hard to the floor, and Benedict saw his old friend, Mr Regan standing there, a bloody knife in his hand.

"You bastard!" Benedict snarled. "You fucking worthless tosser!" He took out his gun and shot the major in the chest.

Regan's face bulged with surprise. His eyes collapsed.

Benedict shot him again, this time in the abdomen.

Regan dropped the knife and fell to his knees before Benedict.

Benedict was about to shoot him for the third time, but then suddenly kicked the officer hard in the stomach. He took away the Regan's gun and held it up. Grimacing ruthlessly, he grabbed the major by the hair and smashed the gun into his face.

Benedict dropped the weapon as Regan fell dead to the floor and examined Captain Simone. He was still alive.

"I'm fine," winced the captain. "Tell the pilots to take off now!"

Benedict left the wounded man and rushed to the command deck. The pilots were already moving the stick around.

"Quickly!" he urged them. "Let's go!"

The pilots moved the ship upwards. The shocked townspeople below were stunned at the fact the *Deviant* had left half the supplies behind. They watched as the hatches were closed and the descending ramp folded in.

Soon, they had passed over the alley and made maximum speed away from the city of Sir Finley.

"We're clear," announced the pilots gleefully.

"I wouldn't say that just yet..." replied Benedict. He pointed at the slaughterers approaching them. They slowed their speeds and suddenly opened a stream of orange fire.

Chapter 11   Slaughterers United

"Fuck!" shouted Benedict as the *Deviant* suddenly dipped. He fell backwards, nearly toppling off his knees. "Shit! Bastards! Bastards!"

The pilots righted the ship, gliding past the slaughterers that had attempted to destroy them. They adjusted the stick as they pulled it up again, away from the terrified townspeople below.

The Omegans opened fire again; this time it hit. Scraps of metal flew off the ship, colliding with people in the markets. More fire poured on them; more shrapnel came off the hull.

Outside, Captain Agathaninon was busy feeling the dull thud as his craft released bullets. He smiled in an inside manner as he broke windows on the *Deviant*. Two Lambdas were seeing cradling their severed limbs.

"It's not enough," the Omegan whispered. He spoke into his intercom. "Slaughterers one to five – attack the bow of the ship with the micro coils; that should prove a bit more effective…"

"Fucking bastards," said Benedict, again realising that he wouldn't be able to shoot them all down. "This has gone far enough…"

"Commander, come and see this."

Benedict went over to the pilots and followed their gazes out the front screen. Five slaughterers had stopped dead ahead of them. They didn't seem to be doing anything, just sitting there.

"What are they doing?" asked Benedict.

The crafts began to release something. It was an almost clear gas, except for slight dull lines, pinpricks in its composition. Coming towards them.

Suddenly the screen cracked slightly, like a tiny rock had been thrown at the glass.

"What was that supposed to be?" remarked Benedict. "It - "

"Help!" screamed one of the pilots. "Help! Help! Help! Help! Help! Heeeeeeeelp!"

Benedict stared mortified as the pilot clutched his throat, choking. He fell to the floor, gagging on white fluid that came pouring through his mouth.

"Get down!" the commander said to the other pilot. "I know what these things are! Keep below the screen!" He bent back down to examine the pilot.

"Heeeeelp!" he croaked. "Heelp…"

"It's all right," said Benedict. "Just keep calm, alright? Take your hands away from your throat." He gently eased off the pilot's fingers and saw the micro coil embedded in the skin. He snatched the pilot's pocket-knife and tried to feed it under the micro coil, but without success.

Suddenly, blood shot out of the pilot's mouth – not liquidly blood, but thick dark blood – the stuff that exists in nightmares. And it leaked out like it had come from a burst bucket, screeching and bleeding and frothing and choking and choking and choking. Then the pilot lay still, save for the remaining slight twitches in his fingers.

"Damn it!" cried Benedict. He hurled himself onto the seat and bravely sat up in it.

"What are you doing?" said the other pilot, now cowering on the floor.

"Piloting the damn ship out of the way," informed the commander. He pulled back the wheel in front of him and the *Deviant* began to lift up, clearing the slaughterers in front. But suddenly there was this growling noise that seemed to originate from the ship's core.

"Change the stick to Mode Two!" cried the pilot.

"What?!"

The pilot picked himself up from the floor and came into closer proximity to Benedict. "Put your foot on the pad and move the stick to Mode Two!" the pilot shouted again.

Benedict looked down to see the pad. He rammed his foot on it.

"No, not like that! *Gently* put your foot on the pad…"

"Okay, I get it!" Benedict *gently* pushed his foot down and reached for the stick, feeling its unearthly grasp. He looked frantically amongst the numbers, trying to see where the 'two' was. He found it – next to the 'one'. He took the stick out of Mode One and flicked it into Mode Two. The growling stopped.

The pilot told him: "Right – slowly lift your foot off the pad."

Benedict began to raise his foot. Suddenly there was this massive whine that shrieked through the ship.

"Not that fast! Slower!"

Benedict pressed the pad back down and very slowly began to release it. There was no horrid whine this time. When, he'd released it he glanced at his temporary 'instructor'.

"Good," said the pilot, "we'll make a pilot of you yet…"

"Oh, thanks…" But suddenly the growling returned. "Let me guess," said the commander. "Put it into Mode Three…"

"Exactly," said the pilot. "Every time there's a massive growl on ascent, do exactly as you've already done."

Benedict repeated the procedure. Somehow, it worked. Then he did it a third time, a fourth, a fifth, and a sixth.

"Right," he said, "what about when I want to stop ascending…?"

"That's a hard part," the pilot informed. "If you are in between Modes, like we are, you have to half-adjust the stick. But since you are a newcomer, press your foot on the pad and then push the wheel forward. Once the ship has levelled, *do* keep your foot on the pad."

"Okay then," said Benedict, about to carry out the instructions. But suddenly, the slaughterers came into view in front of them: every one.

"Shit," muttered the pilot.

"No problemo," said the commander, tapping several buttons on the panel.

"I wouldn't fuck with the weapons systems," said the pilot.

"It's all right," said Benedict, "I had time to study the weapons schematics earlier… I know what I'm doing…"

Suddenly two rockets shot out of the *Deviant*. They streaked their way towards the cloud of slaughterers, burning like asteroids entering the atmosphere.

"Congratulations, Commander," sighed the pilot, grimacing at the panel, and then at him. "You've just released two rubidium warheads."

"Whoops," stuttered Benedict, suddenly throwing forward the wheel. The *Deviant* stooped over, like an old granny slipping on an icy patch with her shopping.

"Are you out of your mind?" screamed the pilot. "You can't just descend a ship like this. You need to be trained first."

"Well what was the alternative?" snapped Benedict. "Sit up there – "

The warheads went off.

Fire filled the sky above them, flames ripping through the heavens like the gods themselves. The slaughterers were vaporised instantly – they hadn't counted on Benedict being at the wheel. But the fire reached further than an average warhead. The people of Sir Finley crouched in fear as the sky above turned orange. Children ran for their moms and fathers ran to seek their families in the confusion.

Meanwhile, back on the *Deviant*, things were even worse – the descent had slowed horribly and there was this horrible sloshing noise originating from the engine. The reason for this was because Benedict had accidentally lifted his foot off the pad, causing the engine to continue the antigravity particle generation; but with the freefall in progress, up and down had clashed. The engine now began to scream like a baby.

"Put your foot back on the pad!" roared the pilot. "Do it now!"

Benedict soon realised his error and thumped his foot back down. Immediately, the freefall became smooth again and the engine stopped its dreadful squeal.

"Fucking hell," said Benedict, quite relieved.

"Right, I suppose you'd better see to Captain Simone," said the pilot.

"Of course," answered Benedict. "I'll leave the piloting to you. Set a course for... well, you know what."

Captain Simone lay in ill health later that day as the unstoppable bleeding continued. His face was devoid of all colours and blood was drooling from his lips.

Gathered around him were Dr Macintyre and Benedict. They both eyed him carefully, in case he wanted anything. But for the moment, all he did was twitch and groan.

"Do you reckon he'll make it?" Benedict asked Dr Macintyre.

"I don't know, Commander. I really don't know."

"What do you mean 'you don't know'? You're supposed to be the fucking doctor around here!"

"Listen to me, Commander," whispered the doctor. "If we were back in England, where I have proper medical equipment, there'd be no problem. As a matter of fact, we're in this crummy little med room with nothing but stencils, calculators and a few bloody vaccines. There's no way of knowing how he'll turn..."

"Well, take his temperature!" Benedict said hoarsely. "You *must* have a thermometer on you somewhere..."

"I have a personal thermometer," said Macintyre, "back in my quarters – but that'll be no use. I don't think the captain has a fever or anything."

"Well, go and get it!" said Benedict. "Come on, let's get *summat* done. Oh, if you're not going to get it, Mr Macintyre, I'll fuck my way down and pick it up for you."

"No!" the captain spat suddenly. "Stay here, Benedict. I have important information."

"I'm right here," said the commander, reassuring the officer. "Doctor," he said to Macintyre. "Get your thermometer and any med supplies you have."

The good doctor grudgingly vanished.

"What is it, captain?"

Simone smiled weakly. "Listen, I have something to give you, Commander. It's very important, so make sure you don't lose it." The captain fiddled around in his pocket and took out a small black box, like a pen case, except slightly smaller.

"What is this?" asked Benedict, his fingers fumbling around the clip.

"Don't open it," said Captain Simone as he shuffled himself on the bed. "You must wait." The captain rubbed his eyes tiredly, obviously quite exhausted.

"Wait for what?" enquired Benedict, still examining the box.

"The right moment – when it comes, you will know when to open the box. You will just know. And when you open that box, you will be able to defeat the enemy."

"What enemy?"

"You will find out," whispered Simone. "You must be patient, not naïve like most young men your age are…"

"You call me naïve," said Benedict. "That's the first time I've heard that word in a long time."

"Well," said Captain Simone lifting his body up and then dropping himself in a seating position, "I am one who's experienced. But I remember those days when I *was* a young naïve individual…"

"Tell me about it," remarked the commander. He meant this as commentary rather than enquiry.

But all the same, Captain Simone responded. "When I was seventeen, I studied creative arts at Glasgow University."

Benedict couldn't help but laugh. An arts student who became a captain in a long lost brotherhood? – yeah right…

"If you're wondering, commander," said Simone as if sensing his thoughts, "I had a bit of a journey getting from that place to here. It's a long story. But anyway, I met this girl also doing my course; Nicole – that was her name. Good God, she was fantastic. One night, everyone on our entire course went out to the boozer and we all got absolutely fucking pissed. Nicole took me back to her flat for some non-alcoholic drinks – well it started as that. You've never shagged a Scotswoman before, Benedict – they're great!"

"And why are you telling me this…?"

"Because it's one of my happy memories," said the captain. "One of my grandest memories. I want you to know it, Benedict; I want you to know it, because I will die soon. And when I die, I want you to pass it on."

"I'll do it," said Benedict, suddenly filled with pity for this man sitting before him. He might've been a stupid, arrogant tosser, but he was one hell of a captain. He was also a survivor. A survivor of the Omega Brotherhood. A survivor of the modern world that changed all the time. He knew deep down that this arrogant tosser wouldn't survive for long.

"Now, listen to me, Commander," said Captain Simone, wiping more sweat from his face. "I would like to apologise for my remarks earlier, when we argued about stopping at Sir Finley."

"It's me who should be apologising," said Benedict. "I was the one who insulted you. I was the bitching bugger, sir."

"No, I should be the one apologising to the man who will be the future."

"What d'you mean – *I'm the future*?"

"Trust me, Benedict," said Simone, placing his hand on the commander's, "you will be." Suddenly he coughed, a thin film of blood appearing on his lips. He wiped it away with his sleeve. "Fuck," he whispered to himself.

"You'll be fine," Benedict did his best to reassure him. "You're a brave fucker, Captain. You'll make it."

"I don't think I will," said Captain Simone. Suddenly, a thick bloody mess came out of his mouth. Tears mixed in with the mess, creating sheer red shit. Benedict placed his hand on the captain's shoulder. More bloody mess vomited out his mouth. The captain struggled briefly then his heart stopped. He lay still.

"Shit," said Benedict. He raised his fingers and ran them over the captain's eyes and shut the lids.

And that was when Dr Macintyre came in with his med kit.

"How's Captain Simone?" he asked.

"He's dead," said Benedict sullenly. He stood up and faced the doctor, enraged. "He's fucking dead!" he vociferated. "He's choked on his own fucking blood!" He saw the med kit. "Why didn't you hurry?" he screamed at Macintyre. "We could've saved him! We could have fucking saved his life! You arrogant bastard, Dr Macintyre. You are a fool – a selfish one at that – sorry, a mistake: you talk with *everyone*, turning them all against me, and into you're armada."

"We are talking about *Captain Simone*!" yelled Dr Macintyre. "Not about your sad little life, okay? Show some respect."

"You're the one who shows no respect."

"Of course I bloody do!"

"For other people, oh yes, but not for me and your other victims."

"Victims?" Dr Macintyre retorted in a furious manner. "How fucking dare you... Who the *hell* do you think you are, my good man?"

"A commander. I'm a commander."

"Don't you dare speak to me like that!" snapped Dr Macintyre. "Don't you ever!"

"This is the point when you expect me to walk away with a dark cloud over my head..." Benedict smiled. "But since we are far beyond the boundaries of the Epsilon Brotherhood, *stick your medical qualifications down your fucking throat!*"

Dr Macintyre backed off. He didn't have security backup with him. He was a villain with all his soldiers depleted. Instead of doing what he always did, he said quietly to the commander:

"If we were back home, I'd have you sentenced to several months – maybe a year – in the worst prison! However, since we are *not* home, I can't do a damn thing – we are under Lambda law." Macintyre walked swiftly out of the room.

"Bastard!" Benedict yelled after him.

Dr Macintyre just glared hatefully at him and then left the room, cursing.

Captain Simone's funeral was later that day. His coffin was carried along the promenade, flowers littering its path and his crew gathered around it.

Benedict and his companions watched tearfully as the box was put on a set of wheels on the exit ramp. A vicar approached the coffin – fully dressed in robes and all – and addressed the crowd with the Lord's Prayer:

"Our Father, who art in Heaven

"Hallowed be thy name

"Thy Kingdom come, thy will be done.

"On Earth as it is in Heaven.

"Give us this day, our daily bread

"And forgive us our trespasses, as we forgive those who trespass against us.

"And lead us not into temptation but deliver us from evil

"For thy is the kingdom, the power, the glory forever and ever.

"Amen."

All before him said "Amen" and then the pilot opened the ramp. The coffin rolled down slope and fell into the clouds.

"Goodbye, Captain," said someone

Chapter 12   A Few Minutes Later

For the next week, the *Deviant* drifted on. They met an occasional straggling slaughterer hanging around. Every so often, they would land the ship so the pilot could have a breather. He would wipe his dirty face of the sweat that lingered on his skin.

All he would ever say is: "Fuck." "Fucking sweat." "That bastard that's God has fucked up my comfort."

Benedict was thoroughly sick and tired of his attitude. He thought – and I thought as well – that this pilot a selfish little –

"Anyway," he said one morning when he and his companions were gathered in the meeting room talking about the mission – but they were all silently grieving about Captain Simone. He seemed to linger in their minds.

"What is it?" said Dr Macintyre, slumped heavily against the dark wall. Sweat was matted against his face, throat, arms. He was tired and exhausted.

Professor Bentley was sitting at the far end of the table. His bowtie was quite undone. His glasses were slung down on the table in front of him. His overcoat was hooked on his chair.

Commander Collington was stood against the door, his Epsilon Uniform same as ever: young and inexperienced.

Bristol was alone in the middle of the lot of them. Her purple hair was tied back behind her head. Her uniform though was still crooked; her face was drooped with a complex matrix of emotions.

"Listen," said Benedict, "with the loss of Captain Simone, I can take it we all feel quite upset – "

"For God's sake, Commander," said the doctor angrily, "we're bloody heartbroken! We're fucking-well totally fucking fucked without our fucking captain!"

"So I take over – which I've just done previously. It's no big deal, Dr Macintyre. It's no big fucking deal at all." Benedict said this with repeated emphasis – he was sick and bloody tired of trying to get Macintyre to understand *anything* he said.

"Very well," said the medic, "if you insist…"

"Yes, I do fucking insist!" Benedict shot back. "We are going to complete this mission – we will take the fortress that Lord Marius abides in. Are we *all* in agreement…?"

"Yes," sniffed Macintyre.

"With you," said Commander Collington.

"I serve faithfully at your side," Professor Bentley said.

Chief Inspector Bristol was hesitant in her response. Gently, she lifted her head and said: "I'm with you."

"Good," said Benedict. "Now, the pilot will take us wherever we need to go. Professor Bentley, is there something wrong?"

"Yes," said the elderly physicist. "I've noticed that all of you seem to be preoccupied with the tactics of fighting and battling – but there's one thing you haven't properly considered: the enemy. The closer we get to their campus, the more harm will be done to us. Have you had time to consider that?"

"Shit," muttered Dr Macintyre, realising that none of them had done so. Dr Bentley had hit the nail on the head. Right bang smack on the head.

"What are we supposed to do?" gasped Commander Collington. "Jesus Christ – why didn't we think about that?"

"There *is* one thing we could do…" said Professor Bentley. "Though it's risky, I dare say it could be done."

"And what would that be?" said Bristol.

"An old friend of mine," explained Bentley. "He lives in eastern Pacifica. Good man, he is: he could send us right into the enemy territory without being detected."

"And how would he do that?" said Macintyre – he was beginning to get quite pissed off with all the false hopes he'd seen over the years – and Bentley was adding another little bit to that wall.

"Experimental teleportation," informed Professor Bentley. "He's experimenting with it."

"Bloody hell," said Benedict. "Sounds like a load of shite, but I suppose it's our best option."

"Are you crazy?" Dr Macintyre said.

"It is," said Benedict, "but the alternative is plunging straight into enemy territory alone – we'd last a few a minutes, maybe an hour."

Bristol was shocked. This 'one night stand' had certainly taken a strange course with his choices.

"How good are his experiments?" said Collington.

"They're reasonably good," said Bentley. "He left the university many years ago to isolate himself here, so he could conduct them in peace."

"I like it," said Benedict, smiling. "Professor, you know the location – tell the pilot to set a course."

"Yes sir," replied Bentley happily. He stood up and left the room.

"You're making a mistake," said Dr Macintyre, following him.

Bristol stared at him briefly, flashing her anger at him. He watched her go, but Commander Collington stayed behind. He was impatient at the moment, his hands quivering ever so slightly.

"What is it?" Benedict asked the young commander when the door had shut and he was sure that they were alone.

Commander Collington was hesitant, but suddenly jumped into his announcement:

"Basically, Benedict, I've got a problem. There's this hot young Lambda officer and she's extremely gorgeous. I want her, Benedict; I want her so much."

Short and brief – but it had the points laid out.

"So what do you want me to do about it?" Benedict replied, sitting himself back down. He took a handful of grapes from the fruit bowl on the table and started munching them, quickly indicating that his friend should do the same. Collington was very slow to respond. But, he sat on the chair opposite Benedict.

"Okay," said Benedict, "how madly are you attracted to her?"

"What do you mean?"

"Sorry," sniffed Benedict, "wrong question: how much are you infatuated by her?"

"You're assuming I'm just *sexually* attracted to her…"

Benedict paused. "Okay, you like her, right?"

"Yeah."

"Very well. Here's the important question: how well do you know her?"

"We only met yesterday," said Commander Collington, unsure of where this conversation was leading to.

"Then how can you love her?" Benedict criticized. "Nope, Mr Collington, you should have a one night stand with her – I think anyway…"

"What are you talking about?" Collington croaked. "Of course I love her…"

"Listen," said Benedict, "on a military mission, if you find an attractive girl and you think you love her, the best way to test it, is to have sex with her. It's the only way, Sonny Jim. Take her to bed, have a bloody good night with her, and then in the morning, you'll know whether you love her or not."

"But, I can't just ask her for sex," Commander Collington said in a hush-hush manner.

"Then you'd better come with me, and we'll find her."

It took them an hour of peering down corridors, stairwells, the lot to find this gorgeous girl.

And she wasn't half gorgeous. She had beautiful streamlined, blond hair that hung loosely. Her face was pale and dotted with freckles. Her eyes were deep blue. She was pretty good-looking.

Pretty good-looking indeed.

"She's alright, isn't she?" smirked Benedict. "God, she'd probably take me through the bloody roof with her looks. She's gorgeous."

"Please," said Commander Collington nervously.

"Well..."

"What?"

"Ask her for sex..."

"But," said Collington, spittle flying off his lips, "as much as I want to, I can't..."

"Oh, go on."

"I'm scared of the consequences."

"What consequences?" cried Benedict. "Come on, we'll go together." He dragged Collington over in her direction. When the girl noticed them, she trotted over.

"What is it?" she asked, smiling with an array of bleach white teeth.

"Go on," encouraged Benedict.

"My dear woman," stuttered the shaky commander. "I would like to express – "

Benedict stamped on his foot, at the same time shouting: "Not like that!"

Collington tried again. But this time, he only let out a slight word: "A – "

"Oh for fuck's sake," said Benedict. He smiled at the girl. "Sweetheart, this gentleman fancies you incredibly. He wants to spend the night with you, so he can discover if he loves you or not."

The officer smiled. She reached out her hand to Commander Collington and took his arm.

"What are you doing?" said the dry mouthed Commander Collington as he was led away.

Benedict watched them disappear. Grimacing to himself, he trudged to his own quarters. He rubbed his eyes due to his tiredness. Another long day. He opened his door and threw himself inside, slamming it behind him.

The first thing he noticed was Bristol sitting on his bed. Her hair was untied this time and her uniform was messed up. She'd been crying.

"How did you get in here?" he shouted. "How the fuck did you get into my quarters?"

"I'm a detective," said Bristol. "I managed to make a key and let myself in. I wanted to tell you something."

"What?"

Bristol cried fresh tears. "I love you, Benedict," she whispered. "I love you."

"I love you too," he said. "But as much as I want to love you, I can't..."

"What do you mean, you can't?" she replied. "I love you, Benedict. And you love me as well. And nothing's gonna fucking change that!"

Benedict lowered his head. And suddenly he was filled with a fresh sense of self. He loved her. He loved her a lot. Nothing could possibly change that.

He sat down next to her and brought her close to him. He kissed her. He kissed her again. He kissed her a third time. Dr Macintyre could do so much damage; he could tell you which shop to go to, when to celebrate, when to dream, but he couldn't tell you how to love.

"I'm so sorry," he whispered to her, tears running down his cheeks. "I'm so fucking sorry. Please forgive me. I've been such a fool – I thought I'd never be able to love again, but there was you. How could I walk away from you...? Not you."

She kissed him again. "Benedict, you're not a criminal. You're the best commander I've ever met; I love you."

He held her face between his hands, brushing away the tears. He couldn't walk away from her – not now; not ever.

They made love for the second time. Benedict felt truly connected to Bristol; she was not just his partner, but his loved one. He cared and loved her with the affection he'd only shown once before to Adeline.

As for the detective, she was discovering not just Benedict but herself as well. She loved that commander, and felt a sense of a long companionship ahead for them both.

They both fell into a lull of deep exploration of the other half.

It was mid-morning when they arrived at their destination: a large farm situated on a central plain in the midst of a tiny collection of grey hills. There was a large farmhouse at the corner of the fields in which an elderly hideaway professor shook with fear when he saw the massive flying machine pass over him and land in a field.

His heartbeat only resumed when he said to himself: "Fucking fucked bends in the laws of physics, however did they manage to build those things?"

He strolled uneasily towards the great ship, seeing its beauty and careful shape gather his mind to a focal point. He glanced with caution as several figures descended down an opening ramp and moved towards him. His heart leaped a second time, when he saw his old friend, Professor Bentley.

But in particular, he noticed the figure with the dark stubble, the dark eyes, the dark aura. He wore the Epsilon symbol on his uniform.

This figure approached him and spoke.

"You must be Professor Winston; I am Commander Nettlefold of the Epsilon Brotherhood – these are my companions: Dr Bentley, as I sure you know, Dr Macintyre, Chief Inspector Bristol – and this is my associate, Commander Collington."

"Well," stammered Winston, "how can I help?"

"Old friend," said Bentley, stepping forward and placing a hand on Winston's shoulder, "we require usage of your teleportation system."

"What?" gasped Professor Winston. "Fucking hell – ooh, sorry. The problem is… the systems are quite experimental. Why?"

"We intend to teleport directly into Omegan territory," said Benedict. "Your teleportation devices would allow us to do so."

"What?!" shouted Professor Winston. "I'm not putting you in Omegan territory. Lord Marius would have my blood head!"

"You'll be paid," said Benedict, ignoring protests from his companions. "Fifty thousand…"

"How many do you want sending in?" Professor Winston enquired.

"Twenty."

"Twenty?!" Winston made it sound more like an exclamation than a genuine question.

"Is there a problem with that?" said Benedict.

"Yes there is: I've only got two hubs – one person apiece. They only work once. They burn out after usage. I don't have enough money to 'magically' create enough hubs to throw half your company into Omegan territory. Maybe, once I have your reward, I can make more hubs."

"Very well," acknowledged Benedict. "Two of us will go."

Commander Collington butted him in the side. "It's not a one-man campaign," he snuffed.

"Of course not!" cried Benedict. "It'll be a two-man campaign. Now, Professor Winston," he continued, "I would be grateful if we could see your miraculous hubs."

The hubs were literally pieces of metal foil embedded in the ground in a humanoid configuration. Sunlight glittered off the studs for hubs that were anchored into the ground with garden nails – garden nails! They weren't even enclosed containers, nor anything save raw earth to lie on. Thick wires connected into both headpieces – that was the only impressive thing about them.

"What are these?" said Benedict, the feeling of grave disappointment arising inside him. He'd come all this way for bastard-all.

"The hubs," explained Professor Winston, trying to sound impressive – but with bastard-all success.

"How do they work?" Professor Bentley asked – at least *he* was eager to find out info about these contraptions…

"Well," said Winston, "the person or people are strapped into the hubs, and we make sure they are - well strapped in tight. The wires that you see travelling into the headpieces deliver a charge of three billion coulombs directly into the candidate. This enables them to be 'protected' by a thing layer of electricity. We then turn on the magnetic expansion devices – or MEDs for short. This theoretically turns them into a string of high frequencies that travel to the location." Winston turned silent.

"That's the biggest load of fucking bollocks I've ever heard!" shouted Benedict.

"It should work," said Professor Bentley. "I've studied all kinds of schematics for teleportation devices – it's all here in these ones."

"Alright," snapped Dr Macintyre, "let's get to the more important business: the plan of action. This is what I propose: Benedict and Commander Collington should teleport to the location. They will distract enemy forces. Then the main armada – led by myself – will jump in and win the day."

"That's a good plan," said Benedict. "We shall commit ourselves to it."

"That's what I like to hear," said Dr Macintyre. "I - "

"Except," interrupted Benedict, "there shall be one minor variation: I will travel in the hubs – along with Dr Macintyre. It shall be Commander Collington who leads the main assault."

"Shit," Dr Macintyre muttered to himself.

"Yes, shit!" said Benedict who'd overheard his private – cough, cough. "Guess we're going to have to cooperate for once… Or are you just a bit too scared of teleportation…?"

"No, I'm not!" retorted the medic. "Okay, both of us."

"Good." Benedict turned to Commander Collington. "Now, my young friend, you are about to take on a large command: are you up to it?"

"Hell yeah!" cried Collington happily – in euphoria.

"Brilliant," said Benedict. "Fucking brilliant. Professor Bentley, return to the *Deviant* and tell the crew to stretch their legs, get some fresh air."

"Sure thing, Benedict," replied the professor, darting off in the direction of the *Deviant*.

"When can you have the hubs ready?" Benedict asked Professor Winston.

"I just need to charge the hubs up," explained the professor. "Shouldn't take more than a few minutes, I don't think."

"Listen, I'm not a physicist or anything, but how do you get three billion coulombs of charge ready in a few minutes?"

"Yeah," Dr Macintyre chimed in. "How d'you do it?"

"It's quite complicated," said Professor Winston. "It'd take hours to explain."

"Oh, alright," said Macintyre, "I've got things to do. If we're going on this mission, I'd better get some med supplies." He began to make his way back to the ship as well.

"Can I have a word with you, Benedict?" said Commander Collington.

"Yeah sure," Benedict replied, knowing exactly what it was about.

"I'll start charging the hubs," said Winston, wanting to get out of the way. He disappeared into the farmhouse.

Benedict waited 'til the professor was truly out of earshot before saying quite loudly to Mr Collington: "Now my good friend, how did it go last night?"

"It went all right," said Commander Collington, brushing his blond hair aside.

"So…"

"So what?"

"Did you fuck her or didn't you?"

"I did," said Collington nervously.

"Hooray!" Benedict said. He felt proud of his friend. Very proud of his friend. "Was it... good?"

"Yeah – it sure was."

"God, you *do* look exhausted!" said Benedict, commenting on the commander's weary face. "She must've given you your best shag in a while."

"Indeed she did." Collington glanced over his shoulder, making sure that Professor Winston wasn't eavesdropping on them. "But... No, nothing."

"But what?"

"No – it's nothing."

"Just tell me!"

"Well – there was this bit when she went on top and – no, I won't tell."

"Yes, you will."

"Well, she started..."

"Come on."

"She started..."

"Tell me."

"She started... screaming."

"What's so bad about that?" cried Benedict. "It's when she does nothing that you have to think about your choice of companion – in the new sense of the word."

"Well, some of the folks next door might have heard it."

"Oh, come on! What's to worry about that?"

"They'll pass comments behind my back," said Commander Collington.

"No they won't! They were probably doing the exact same thing, you know. In fact, they were probably jealous of you. You – with my help – chatted up the most gorgeous girl on the ship. You – where did you have sex with her?"

"My quarters."

"You took this gorgeous crackpot back to your quarters and shagged her. All they probably managed to do was have a night with the dregs of modern society. You took today's equivalent of – what *was* she called? – the Prom Queen, and had sex with her. At most, they're probably going to say how they envy you behind your back."

"I suppose so," said Collington.

"Now, my good friend, you may consider a long term relationship with her."

"I think so," said Commander Collington.

"My friends!" shouted Professor Winston, coming out of the farmhouse. "The sweethearts are fully charged. I'm finalising the connections." He popped back inside.

"Good; Mr Collington, go and get Dr Macintyre for me would you? And tell the others to prepare for takeoff – you're leaving now."

"Yes, Benedict."

"Mr Collington, one more thing."

"Yes?"

"You're a good man," said Benedict, beaming at his friend. "Over the past weeks I've watched you develop. You're on the way to becoming a great general. And now you may have found your woman, your lifelong companion. I wish to tell you this now, Justin, because you need to leave now. As soon as Dr Macintyre is here, both of us shall leave, at the same time as you depart. I just wanted to say that it has been the greatest privilege of my life to serve at your side and see you develop yourself into a better man than I am ever capable of being myself."

He reached out his hand and shook Collington's.

"I'll see you in Omegan territory," said the young commander.

"You as well," said Benedict, releasing Collington.

The young commander, a friend of Benedict, trudged back towards the ship. In the other direction came Dr Macintyre, a brand new white coat strung on his shoulders. He carried his med kit at his side in a small leather bag.

A few minutes later, there was a sucking sound as the *Deviant* lifted off the ground. It hovered there for a few seconds, and then flew forward, ascending into the clouds.

Commander Collington was gone.

"Right then," said Dr Macintyre. "I've got everything." He was examining his med supplies, checking all the creams.

"Professor Winston," said Benedict, "are we ready to rock and roll?"

"Yes, we are," said the estranged Winston. "Ready when you are."

Benedict took out his pistol briefly, and then put it back in his holster. "Okay," he said, "Dr Macintyre – ready? Let's go."

Chapter 13   Teleportation

Benedict shivered as Professor Winston pulled the last leg strap tight. He felt the blood get cut off in all his limbs. But his heart stammered with fear even more when Winston put the metal helmet onto his head. The professor smiled at him and whispered: "It won't hurt a bit."

"That's quite reassuring," said the commander, glancing across to Dr Macintyre who had already been plugged in.

"Looks like he's ready," said Professor Winston, following Benedict's stare. "Right, finished. Let's get this party started. What singer said that?"

Winston vanished back into the farmhouse, shouting behind him: "Good luck guys!"

"Thanks for the encouragement," whispered Dr Macintyre.

"It'll be all right," said Benedict, glad once again to be reassuring the medic. "You are gonnae be just fine."

"Stop imitating my vaguely Scottish accent," Macintyre shot at him.

"You didn't tell me you were a jock," said Benedict. Of course, he'd noticed Dr Macintyre's occasional Scottish accented language *and* his sometimes old Scottish words like 'bonny' and 'oldae'. And of course the most infamous one: 'cun – '

Nope. Better not go there with that one.

Suddenly Professor Winston shouted at them: "I'm ready! Are you?"

"Yes!" both Benedict and Dr Macintyre replied.

"Good!" responded the professor. "Switching you on – now…"

Benedict felt his mind burn.
Burn with fire.
Fire.

Fire that burned.

Fire burning in Benedict's mind.

He felt his whole sense of self slip into fire. Fire that burned with an orange, crackly scent. Like the scent of a wood fire in a cosy log cabin. He was sitting on a comfy armchair reading a Charles Dickens book. There was a cup of tea in a traditional china teacup. He was so homely, a homely place with pictures on the walls and...

... the shearing pain! Fire in his heart! Fire in his body! Fire in his mind!

He was travelling.

In three dimensions. He was travelling in space.

In four dimensions. He was travelling in time.

In *five* dimensions. He was travelling in –

He was falling through holes. Then he fell through a wormhole.

He was burning.

Burning with fire.

Fire.

Fire that was burning.

Fire that burned him.

Then he was in another house. It had two armchairs side by side next to a fireplace. And a bookshelf. And a door.

"Well, bloody hell," said Benedict, making his way to the window. "I'm home!" Outside the sun was shining. The fields were lit up. And the bloody farmer was grumbling as he picked up straw from a spill obviously caused by his repeatedly overturning cart.

"Dr Macintyre! Are you here as well?" He didn't want the medic in his house.

"No, he's not," said someone.

Benedict spun around to see a dark figure sitting in one of the armchairs. This figure was smoking a thin cigarette, releasing a thin stream of wispy smoke.

"Who the fuck are you?" Benedict said. "Get out of my house!"

"This isn't your house," said the figure.

"Yes it fucking is!"

"This is a duplicate of your house," said the figure, puffing out more smoke, "in a place beyond your wildest dreams. Welcome to the other side of the universe, Benedict."

"Don't be fucking ridiculous!" snapped the commander. "You're an alchy who's found the keys in front of my doorstep and made himself at home here."

"It's not your home."

"Sure it is," said Benedict. He opened the latch on his window. "Let's get some fresh air in here." He swung open the glass.

And got the shock of his life.

Below was some sort of encampment.

Not an encampment.

Hundreds, thousands of beds, stretching onto the red horizon. The sun was dying. The mountains were dying. And on those beds was… pain.

And there was this massive noise… Screaming! Shouting! Shoving!

"Fuck." One word that Benedict muttered to himself. "What the hell is this place?"

"Welcome," said the figure approaching him from behind. "This is a place of science. A place of experimentation."

"Some experiment," said Benedict. "This is like a massive fucking whorehouse."

"There is eternal joy here," said the figure. "Many species of people across the universe are deprived of love – we give it to them. You yourself are deprived of love. Now you can enjoy it forever…"

And then the house disappeared.

Benedict was standing alone on a mountain overlooking the massive experiment.

And suddenly a white light appeared in his eyes. He was flung into it, turning corners, up and down.

And hit the grass extremely hard.

"Ow," sniffed the commander, expecting to be greeted by some beautiful-looking whore. But instead, he found himself standing in a rainforest. Looking down, he saw the smoke rising off his uniform. His gun was there.

Suddenly there was this hissing sound and Dr Macintyre appeared in front of him, hitting the ground with a crack.

"You all right?" said Benedict to the medic.

"Fine," said Dr Macintyre, jumping to his feet. "That was the oddest sensation I've ever felt. I went somewhere – oh, it doesn't matter. I'm fine now."

"Not for much longer," said a voice from in the trees. *Another* elderly professor entered the scene; he was carrying a shotgun in his arms. "Take out your gun and toss it to the side," he ordered. "Now."

Benedict threw away his gun, so did Macintyre.

"Who the hell are you?" Benedict enquired.

"Professor Davenport," said the man. "You killed my friend Major Regan, didn't you, Benedict. Oh yes, I know you – you little bastard. Arms up."

Benedict began to raise his arms, but suddenly swung sideways and knocked the gun from Davenport's arms.

"Fuck!" snarled the professor as Benedict punched him in the face.

"No – fuck you, ya little cunt!" screamed Benedict, kicking him in the bollocks. "I've had enough wankers to deal with for one fucking day! Enough!" He punched again.

"Shit!" replied the prof. But it was not a shout of pain, but a shout of being betrayed. Davenport was wincing with hate as he ripped of his face.

And underneath was a young blond woman. Blood was drooling down her jaw, from Benedict's punching. Now the commander wished he'd never hurt her at all.

"Fuck me," was all he could say. "Fuck me big fucking time. I'm such a fucking – "

"Enough of the swearing," said the woman. "All right, love? Don't worry, I used a voice box." This was directed not at Benedict, but at Dr Macintyre who was stood back quite shocked.

"My dear," said the medic, "what are you doing out here? You should be at home, sweetheart… Not here in this most ghastly place!"

"Well, I'm here," said the girl.

"But why?" said Benedict, mystified. "I thought – "

"You're not my hubby," said the girl. "You've been told to keep away from me."

"Oh, come on!" cried Benedict. "I'm not trying to marry you again; I just want to see how you're doing these days. I'm not wanting to suck your cunt anymore."

"I'm fine," said Adeline, obviously quite disgusted at this comment. "Just fine. More interested in Dr Macintyre – oh, my sweet Philip!" she beamed, rushing towards the doctor and pressing her mouth against his. It wasn't a kiss – it was more of a sexual sucking of his lips, trying to rip them off his face.

"Can you two just stop that?" said Benedict, quite disgusted. "We've got a war to win here."

"What war?"

This was said by Lord Marius who was entering the scene with twenty soldiers, all armed to the teeth.

"Shit," gasped Benedict in more of a mutter than anything. "I didn't guess that we were being spied upon…"

Lord Marius swept his look of pride around them all, saying finally to the commander: "Welcome to the land of the Omega Brotherhood, my good old friend, Benedict."

Benedict strained for the third time as he tried to shake off the chains, but clearly without any success at all. His arms were sore, his stomach was sore, and he just wanted to go home, back to his sad little cottage – well it wasn't that sad: quite comfortable compared to the rubbish dump that he was currently imprisoned in.

Next to him Dr Macintyre was exactly the same. He was sick and tired of this adventure that had supposed to be one, but had instead turned into a bloody nightmare.

And now they were stuck in a filthy, vomit-stricken cell with dead corpses in the corner. They weren't the bleach-white skeletons that you read in adventure books, but dirty rotting corpses – some of them were still biologically active. Blood was dripping off their bald skulls, turning the stone floor into a complete filthy mess.

Adeline had been taken elsewhere when they arrived at the fortress. Dr Macintyre was worried about her; but Benedict wasn't that scared for her: after how she'd believed the medic when he'd ruined his wedding and how she went on to marry that selfish brat, he didn't give a hoot.

Besides, Lord Marius wasn't that bad. Before he'd turned Omegan, he was a very beneficial man to the Epsilons. He'd done more than Benedict had. Of course, now he was upset at the fact his chief scientist had been found out to be a tranny; but maybe later he would lighten up and then he and Benedict could have a nice drink together.

He would be very surprised that one of his advisors was a traitor...

"Damn," said Dr Macintyre, fiddling again with the chains that held them both to the wall.

"Nothing good'll come from that," remarked Benedict. "You may as well do a spot of lap dancing instead."

"It's not funny," said Dr Macintyre. "This is a serious life threatening situation for both of us – "

"For you maybe," Benedict interjected. "Not for me though. Lord Marius and I happen to have been acquainted."

"I bet it was at a party of some sort," Dr Macintyre laughed. "You both got a bit drunk – "

"If I was out of these chains," said Benedict in a sinister manner, "I'd break your fucking neck."

Suddenly the great iron door opened. Lord Marius entered with Adeline at his side. She was crying.

"Evening all," said the lord. Adeline suddenly screamed and bitch-slapped Lord Marius. Enraged, he threw Adeline to the floor. She hit the hard stone with a sickening crack. "Take that, you fucking whore," he spat at her, wiping the blood from his mouth.

"Why did you do that?" cried Dr Macintyre, watching his fiancé creep up from the floor in pain.

"That little bitch infiltrated my fortress," said Lord Marius.

"She wouldn't do such a thing," Dr Macintyre said defensively.

"Well you *would* say that, wouldn't you?" Lord Marius raised his upper lip at him. "Hmm? You bastards in the medical always make your jargon up. Oh, you always screw things up for other folk. That's what your job is. In fact, I can say I'm almost jealous of it: you get to bugger around with other peoples' lives, then talk to writers and poets, saying how 'interesting' everything is. Then you return to your office and screw other peoples' lives up again."

"Well, I wouldn't put it like that..." stuttered Macintyre.

"Yes – I would," said Lord Marius. He seemed to show a slight fear in his eyes at this defiance. "And let *me* tell you summat, mate: I think that I should shoot Miss Paulington here." He took out his gun and put it to her head. "But I'm not – because, she means something to my friend Benedict over there. I don't hate Epsilons – I just hate their medical core." He removed a control from his pocket and pointed it at Benedict.

The commander felt himself being released from the restraints. He nearly collapsed to the ground, but steadied himself. He saw Lord Marius hand Benedict's gun down to him.

"Thank you," said the commander, taking the weapon. "I am with you – on your side, sir."

"Traitor!" Dr Macintyre accused out loud. "Benedict – you treacherous bastard!" But then the good doctor was quite surprised when Lord Marius released him as well.

Macintyre trotted slightly in a circle, waiting for the dizziness to go, and he was eventually stable.

"Let me take a good look at you," said Lord Marius, examining the young doctor who stood defiantly before him. "You're a youngan. You've got a promising relationship with Adeline ahead of you – sorry, *had* a promising relationship…"

"What are you talking about?" said Dr Macintyre. "What the fuck are you talking about?"

"In this gun," Lord Marius informed, holding up his weapon, "are seven bullets containing Average Joe's gunpowder – but there's one: a bullet containing a bacterial agent that's been… mutilated by my black light. You'll die a most horrid death, Mr Macintyre."

"*Dr* Macintyre," stressed the medic.

"Not for much longer," sneered Lord Marius, firing once.

Dr Macintyre fell back, his eyes screaming with pain. He pulled himself back up again, but suddenly the blood began pouring out from the bullet wound in his chest.

It came pouring out like… it was screaming! The blood was *screaming*. It was screaming and screeching out of his body, spewing out like a burst water fountain.

Suddenly Dr Macintyre's head arched back and blood started… gagging out of his mouth. At first red, but then… darker… and darker. And suddenly it was coming out black as oil. And just as viscous. There were bits in it, parts of his gut… And they were red against the dark blood.

"Hah!" screamed Lord Marius gleefully. "Look out you now, you bastard!"

Suddenly he bulged forward and vomited… his lungs. They didn't come out fast, but he choked them out slowly, choked out two large bulging objects, like they were being born from his mouth. They came out red and bloody and liquidly.

His heart! It started to come out of his mouth. Pressing between his teeth, it was still beating. Then Macintyre's uncontrollable jaw dropped…

"Heeeeeeelp," he managed to croak, raising his head up. All his face was bloody with the thick dark blood.

Lord Marius was laughing wildly. "Not so happy now, are you?" Marius shouted. "Just fuckin' die, you worthless little bastard!"

And suddenly his lips started to slacken and they… came off. Then his face fell apart, his skin collapsing into the mess on the floor. His legs buckled, the bones cracking like bangers. Then the wonderful Dr Macintyre fell – quite literally – into the pile of death.

Silence fell throughout the room.

Benedict stared in disgust at the remnants. His worst enemy had died.

"Phew," said Lord Marius, staring down at the mushy remains. "Good Heavens on Earth, I thought I'd never get rid of that little bugger. Take that you motherfucker!" he suddenly shouted.

"I'm not impressed," said Benedict. "I wanted to kill that bastard – I didn't want you to do it, sir."

"But I wanted you to enjoy the show," protested Lord Marius. "Come on – admit it…"

"I'll admit this," Benedict replied, taking out his gun.

"What d'you think you're doing?" snarled Lord Marius.

Benedict shot him. Once in the chest; once in the stomach. "Fuck you," he whispered to the lord. "Fuck you big fucking time."

"What the fuck are you doing?" gasped the collapsed Omegan.

"Killing you, that's what I'm doing, you motherfucker," said Benedict.

And with a third bullet he shot Lord Marius through the head.

"Benedict," said Adeline from where she was at the back of the cell. "My God, Benedict." She approached him and slapped him hard. "You cunt!" she screamed. "You tosser! You could have saved Dr Macintyre! You could have saved my hubby-to-be!"

Benedict, seemingly ignoring her, replaced his gun and attempted to walk past her. But she blocked his path.

"Get out of my way," he said, quite infuriated.

"No."

Benedict shouted: "Get out of my way, you fucking bitch! Or you'll end up like them back there." He jerked his thumb backwards, and then pushed his way past her. He'd just walked a few feet, when he heard a gunshot.

Retracing his steps, his heart nearly fell out of his ribcage.

Adeline had shot herself through the head.

Chapter 14 Black Light

"Adeline!" cried Benedict, tears flowing down his cheeks and onto his uniform. "Oh, Adeline! My sweet..."

But she was well and truly dead. She'd put the gun to her chin... and fired. Blood soaked through her dusty hair.

Benedict fell to the ground, picking up Adeline's dead body and pressing his face into hers. "No!" he screamed. "Shit. Oh, fuck! I'm sorry Adeline – oh, darling, I'm so fucking sorry! Not you! Oh, fuck. Shit. I've hurt you, just like I hurt everyone else. Adeline. *Adeline*!"

"Get up, mate," said a voice behind him. "Drop the gun, and get on your feet!"

"Alright," said Benedict, initially calmly, but then, "I've had enough voices behind my back for one day..." He spun around and fired his gun – every round, catching the guard in the throat.

Two other guards who heard the commotion dashed down the corridor to see what all the fuss was about, but were confronted by Benedict who had just reloaded his gun. They yelped as bullets smashed into their skulls, killing them instantly.

"Bastards," the commander spat out loud, pushing himself passing the dead corpses. He spotted a fourth guard who was attempting to alert the others. Swearing heavily, he shot him, watching as the guard screamed his dying words and fall to the floor.

More death.

But he didn't stop there: picking up Lord Marius's and Dr Macintyre's weapons, he started a rampage through the fortress – killing all who lay in his path, he was not an Epsilon Commander, but something else: a killer.

No soldier in that fortress could stand up to him. Some begged him for mercy, some tried to seek help, and some tried to fight him, but he just ploughed his way past them.

A few of them tried to set up two lines of infantry, trying desperately to knock Benedict down. They opened fire, the shots echoing down the hallway, crashing into the walls, splattering bits of paint onto the floor.

The commander jumped down, hiding behind a small statue – one of Lord Marius, of course... He waited a few seconds, as he reloaded his weapons, and then rolled out, releasing bullets. Both ranks dropped dead by the time he'd reached the other side of the corridor.

Benedict stood up, in deep admiration of what he'd done.

"That's payback time, fellas," he snuffed. But one of the men had survived, cradling his injured leg. Benedict approached the fearful man who had tears sodden on his lips, cringing in fear. The commander lowered his gun and shot and shot.

"Take that, you little bastard," he said.

Suddenly more guards appeared. "Get that little cunt!" one of them cried.

So Benedict raised his guns and fired, killing more men. He killed and killed. Blood and blood and blood. So much blood.

And he finished that bloody campaign, dead men forming a black-red trail behind him. Fucking scum. That's what they were. Worthless fucking scum.

Thinking, he had finished, he was surprised at himself: an unfinished job. He heard noises from a nearby room – noises of an unfinished job. Cursing at himself, he opened the door of the castle whorehouse.

And resumed his killing...

He finished when he was sure all of them were dead – not just the whorehouse, but the entire castle: the maids, the servants, the physicists... He killed the lot like animals.

And he eventually completed his bloody massacre.

Sickened with himself, he walked calmly out of the fortress and trudged up the hill, finding a place to sit on a clump of rocks. He wouldn't need Commander Collington or the Lambdas – he'd killed the bastards (all of them) himself.

"Fuck," he whispered to himself. "Fuck me." He cried again. "Fuck me big time." Suddenly he wept out loud. "Jesus Christ! God damn it. God damn myself; what the fuck I have I done?! I've killed so many! I've even killed... whores!"

But there was no time to grieve.

Suddenly, the castle below shimmered. Shimmered with black. Black light.

"Fuck," said Benedict.

The windows darkened as whatever it was filled the fortress. It was liquid but seemed without mass, almost vapour. It began to pour out the windows, filling the gardens.

The commander was alarmed. He checked all three of the pistols for ammo. Macintyre's was empty. So was Lord Marius's. His own one still had bullets lodged inside.

Smiling, he tossed the others away and pointed his gun and the black shimmer.

Would these bullets work though?

Captain Simone!

Fumbling inside his uniform, Benedict removed the black box. Opening it, the glitter sparkled his imagination. It must have been some kind of special bullet, because it inspired those shut off corners of his imagination that he had thought sealed long ago.

Quickly, he loaded his gun with the special bullet and spun the barrel, aiming it at the shape...

... only to find it knock him to the ground.

"Shit!" he cried as the gun fell out his hand. It clattered to the floor.

And the dark shape swung at him again, knocking the commander further a field. He frantically searched for his weapon.

Couldn't find it.

"Fuck!" Benedict dodged out of the way as the black light struck down at him again. "Shit!"

Then Bristol appeared. In her thin detective uniform, she was a pin against a knife. "Here, Benedict," she said, handing him his gun.

Benedict threw himself to his feet, aimed the gun, pulled back the lever, and fired.

The entire universe seemed to stand still as the bullet exploded outwards…

… and struck the black light.

It stopped too.

It stopped dead still.

And then the shadow fell to pieces.

Blasting itself into tiny fragments…

… that pulsated briefly…

… before *dying*…

… and dying…

Dead.

Benedict dropped the gun. Relieved, he fell backwards, into the arms of Bristol.

"Hey, it's okay," she whispered. "You saved the world today, darling."

"Of course I did, love," he replied. "It's me job." He allowed the detective to help him up. He kissed her briefly, before bending down to pick up his weapon.

Suddenly Bristol screamed. A surviving Omegan stood several feet away. Holding a gun – a typical rifle of the Omega Brotherhood. He aimed it. He fired.

Bristol staggered as the bullet crashed into her chest.

"Noooooooo!" Benedict yelled so loudly that it caused the Omegan to stumble backwards, dropping the gun. The commander was so enraged that he shot blindly at the enemy.

The Omegan was struck in the throat. Black viscous blood shot out his neck. And he fell to the ground. Choking.

"You cunt!" he shouted at the corpse. He fell down next to Bristol and cradled her in his arms. She was still alive – but barely.

"It's all right," he whispered to her. "It's all right."

"I love you," Bristol whispered back. "I love you, Benedict."

"And I love you too," said the commander. "And *you* are going to be fine. Okay?" Tears crept out of his eyes. "You are going to be fine, darling."

She struggled in his arms briefly.

"I'm so sorry I hurt you," he said.

"You didn't hurt me," said Bristol. "You loved me more than anyone's ever loved me before. You saved me."

"You *saved* me," he contradicted. "Through all these adventures, through good places *and* bad places, I thought I'd never find you – but I did."

"And I found you." A tear fell down her cheek.

"Come on, darling – love of my life. I love you, Rachel." Benedict released more tears.

She quivered, trying to stay awake. More tears rolled down her cheeks. She held so strongly onto Benedict. As quick as she had love him, she shut her eyes forever.

"No!" Benedict cried. "No! Not her! Oh, fuck – fuck! Oh please, God, you bastard! Give her back to me!" He wept over her. "No! Oh please… Shit. Shit, fucking shit!"

The *Deviant* appeared overhead, a great hulking mass of pride. It put out the landing struts and parked on the edge of the hill, a short distance away from Benedict.

Commander Collington was the first out, cocking his gun, followed by Professor Bentley and the pilot. Soldiers followed.

"What is it?" Collington enquired nervously as he approached them. He soon saw the scene and rushed to Benedict's side. "I'm so sorry," he whispered, putting a hand on the commander's shoulder.

Professor Bentley and the pilot darted over. The elderly physicist held her head and howled like a wolf.

All four of them grieved so fiercely.

Another good person had died that day.

King Christopher and his royal aides arrived later that day on the *Champion*. As this ship was the pride of the fleet, the engines were much more powerful and the pride of the fleet was nearby to Pacifica, it arrived pretty quickly.

They landed adjacent to the *Deviant*, like two neatly parked cars. The ramp opened and the royal figures descended down the ramp. They were expecting a warm welcome of feast and champagne – so imagine their surprise when they saw a whole load of sorry souls gathered together in a rough formation to greet them…

King Christopher and his assistant, the Patrician, were quite disappointed when they saw it. The king recognised Commander Collington and Professor Bentley; but where were the others? And who were these people wearing the Lambda symbols?

Questions. Questions.

But without answers.

At least not yet.

King Christopher approached Collington and asked: "Where's the Minuet?"

"He's dead, Majesty," replied the commander.

"Then I demand to speak with General Mickson," said King Christopher. Behind him the Patrician had removed his cocaine box and was taking a sniff of the white powder. It seemed to rattle him a bit. The Patrician *was* a bit of an addict – but no one dared to tell him that to his face.

"General Mickson's dead too, Majesty."

"Well – who else is dead?"

"All the Epsilon soldiers, Majesty, along with Tame, Sender, Dr Macintyre, and… Bristol." Collington quickly swept a tear from his eye. "Apologies, Your Majesty."

"It is all right," said the king. "What about Commander Nettlefold – is he around? I have his stripes with me." He held up a velvet case.

"He's over that way," said Commander Collington, "Your Majesty." He flashed anger at the king as he made his way into the bushes, accompanied by the Patrician.

"God-awful mess down there," commented the king, indicating the mass of rubble that had come off the castle when the black light burst into existence.

"Of course it is, sir," replied the Patrician.

They found Benedict sitting by himself, quite alone: the body of Bristol had been taken away and stored on the *Deviant*. He winced lightly when he saw His Majesty; he appropriately stood, especially when he saw the Patrician.

"Good day, Your Majesty, Mr Patrician," he said, bowing deeply.

"I'd like to congratulate you on your mission," said the king, shaking hands with the commander. "It has been hard, for all of you, and you performed your duty to your utmost ability. I think the Patrician would like to condole you on your own efforts."

"Indeed sir," said the Patrician; he too shook hands with Benedict.

"Thank you, Mr Patrician." Benedict bowed low again.

"And now to reward you for your efforts," said His Majesty, removing the velvet package, "your general's stripes. Allow me..." He removed the prize from its package and attached it around Benedict's wrist. "I hereby instate you as..." He fastened the stripe... "*General Benedict Nettlefold. Congratulations.*" He shook hands again with Benedict.

"Thank you, Your Majesty," said Benedict, and, knowing the correct procedures, bowed and exited the scene.

The *Champion* and the *Deviant* raced each other home, pilots on both ships enjoying this 'leisurely' flying for the first time.

Professor Bentley was on the command deck of the *Champion* with the king and the Patrician, enjoying the scenic views. He'd also managed to acquire a new set of clothes and looked a good gentleman with his neckerchief, white coat, etc.

Commander Collington had decided to stay on-board the *Deviant*... with that new girlfriend of his. They were shagging pretty much every second. Obviously, he *had* found someone. Benedict was proud of him.

Ah! As for the general, he sat alone in his new quarters aboard the *Champion*. He couldn't stand the Lambdas – they were too full of adventure now – no, he much preferred being with the cynical but all right Epsilons.

He sat hunched on his bed, looking at a photograph of Bristol. She had loved him so much. And now she was dead. She had reached out of the darkness for him, like only Adeline had done before Dr Macintyre had ruined him.

Oh, that little infidel had crippled the then commander, stripping him of those precious stripes and that precious wife. And now he had those stripes, but it wasn't the same. Not without a wife. And Bristol would have been that wife, but no: some bastard from the Omega Brotherhood took her away from him.

So they flew on.

Chapter 15   Home

Benedict was the first to step off the *Champion* when it arrived at the airport. A seething crowd of sightseers, and fans gathered to welcome him.

But he didn't feel like a hero.

There had been so much blood on that mission, that heroism wasn't part of anything anymore. He had gone out as a man searching for his general's stripes, and came back with them – but on that journey he had lost his most precious possession: Bristol. She had been taken from him.

He was wearing his freshly-cleaned uniform and nicely polished shoes that glimmered in the evening sun, watching as the *Deviant* landed close by.

A young girl of about twelve years managed to push past one of the coppers holding back the crowd and approached Benedict with a basket of flowers. The copper saw this and attempted to push the girl back into the crowd, but Benedict waved his hand, indicating that the girl should be allowed to come forward.

"Welcome home, General," she said feebly.

"Thanking you, love," he replied, taking the flowers off her: typical undergrowth from Essex – but that was homely for Benedict. He kindly escorted the girl back into the crowd.

And suddenly there was a massive applause – not for the king, or the Patrician, but solely for Benedict. It rang on through the entire gathering. The newly-instated general turned around to see that it wasn't just the crowd, but the entire crew of the *Champion*, the *Deviant*, the royalties, and Commander Collington and Professor Bentley.

And just to think that when he'd last stood here, he was despised and disgraced and left out; but now, he was loved by everyone. He glanced up at Commander Collington and his new girlfriend. God – she *was* alright!

And Bentley was standing nearby. A true professor, of course…

"Who gave me all this reputation?" Benedict asked himself.

"No time to ask questions!" announced the king. "I believe you have the right to make speech…"

"Certainly," said Benedict, standing right before the crowd. "I went on this mission," he told them, "in the hope of finding my stripes – but I found more than that; I lost more than that. Sometimes we all have these experiences. And it's what we lose that can finish someone off. I lost someone that I loved," he continued. "I loved her, and I lost her. And then I remembered that this is war, a war takes lives. We have to accept that." He suddenly flashed anger at the king. "But Rachel Bristol wasn't a soldier. She was a detective, and because of the royalties we have, she was cast far from her home… on her *debut* mission! She shouldn't have been sent. And now she's dead. She was a young woman with a prosperous future… with me. She's never going to be able to love again. I wish it could've been me who was shot; I was nothing compared to her. I'd do anything to give her a second chance at life. She deserves a second chance more than King Christopher deserved his royal mixture of food. That's all I wish to say." He walked through crowd.

King Christopher watched troubled as the commander vanished. "Well, I wouldn't put it *quite* like that folks…"

As Benedict journeyed home in a cab, he thought about his adventure. Well, it was hell of a trip! Bloody hell, it was!

He past familiar sights and people, but at the same time he missed people from the adventure, sadly including Dr Macintyre. Would he ever experience something like that again? Perhaps. It would be great though.

But he hadn't time to think about anything, because the cab pulled up in front of his cottage. He got out, paid the driver, and approached his front door.

As the cab pulled away, he noticed there were several people behind him. Nervously, he took out his gun and spun around.

The four youths were there with their metal rods. One of them stood forward, a grin on his face.

"Bloody hell, Rob!" said Benedict, embracing his friend.

"Aye, it's good to see you!" Rob responded, shaking the general by the hand. "Congratulations to you, mate: you're home and you've got your stripes!"

"Thank you, mate."

"Listen: got to go," Rob informed him. Almost immediately, he and his friends dashed to a nearby car. They shot off down the country roads.

Benedict suddenly realised that his door was open.

It was true.

That mysterious man must've been there.

The man from the vision. The vision of pain. The world of pain.

Benedict put forward his gun and cautiously trod into his home. Then he realised he was incredibly stupid, because sitting in one of his armchairs was his friend John, who was quite asleep.

"John!" cried Benedict, rushing to greet his friend.

"God, bastard!" John shouted, waking up, shaking Benedict's hand. "You must have thought I was an intruder, 'cos you came in here with a face as blank as salt. You asked me to come in here occasionally, 'cos – Benedict, what's wrong?"

"Rachel's dead," he said, sitting on his armchair. "I met her on the mission; I loved her and she loved me. She's fucking dead, John. Shot by one of those Omegan motherfuckers."

"Oh, shit – I'm sorry, Benedict. I'm bloody sorry."

"It's all right, John. She was a good woman, and I'll always remember," he replied, suddenly thinking about the lovemaking. The smoothness of her skin, the tenderness of her breasts, the –

"I've got me general's stripes," Benedict said in an effort to forget.

"Bloody hell!" cried John, patting him on the shoulder. "This deserves celebration! Right, I'll put the kettle on then."

"That's a right good idea," said Benedict.

There was a knock on the door. Benedict said, "I'll get it!" and made his way to the cottage entrance. He got quite a surprise when he saw a copper standing there, a battered uniform and helmet before him.

The policeman firstly said: "May I congratulate you on your recent success, general."

"Thank you," replied Benedict, most shocked. "Can I help you, mate?"

"Yes, you can," said the copper. "Got a bit of a problem, sir: since you've been gone, the crime's gone up exponentially. In particular, there's this one little gentleman, name of Park, who's been a right little bastard, sir – if you'll excuse the language."

"It's all right, mate, I've heard worse. Well what do you want *me* to do?"

"Can you take him out or arrest him for us, mate?" said the copper. "You'd be bloody brilliant if you did that."

"Well..." said Benedict. He took out his gun and spun the barrel. "How much?"

"A thousand – the team's desperate."

Benedict smiled. "Alright then." He put the gun into his coat. "Let's get started – it's six already."

Lightning Source UK Ltd.
Milton Keynes UK
UKOW02n0744071216
289319UK00003BA/17/P